Anonymous

Life and Services of General U.S. Grant

conqueror of the rebellion, and eighteenth President of the United States

Anonymous

Life and Services of General U.S. Grant
conqueror of the rebellion, and eighteenth President of the United States

ISBN/EAN: 9783744731201

Printed in Europe, USA, Canada, Australia, Japan

Cover: Foto ©Raphael Reischuk / pixelio.de

More available books at **www.hansebooks.com**

LIFE AND SERVICES

OF

GENERAL U. S. GRANT,

CONQUEROR OF THE REBELLION,

AND

EIGHTEENTH PRESIDENT OF THE UNITED STATES.

"WE HAVE WHIPPED THEM ONCE, AND I THINK WE CAN DO IT AGAIN."—*Grant at Belmont.*

This Life of GENERAL GRANT has been compiled from the most authentic sources, and is published under the authority of the Republican National and Congressional Committees. The undersigned are responsible for all statements of facts that it contains.

W. E. CHANDLER,
Secretary Republican National Committee.
T. L. TULLOCK,
Secretary Republican Congressional Committee.

PHILP & SOLOMONS, WASHINGTON, D. C.
1868.

Stereotyped
By McGill & Witherow,
Washington, D. C.

LIFE OF GENERAL GRANT.

CHILDHOOD OF GRANT.

Ulysses, eldest child of Jesse R. and Hannah Grant, was born on the 27th of April, 1822, at Point Pleasant, an obscure town in what was then the far-western State of Ohio. His parents were well-to-do people, furnished with as large a supply of this world's goods as any of their neighbors, and both able and willing to afford him all the advantages of education then attainable at so great a distance from the Atlantic coast. His father was of direct Scottish lineage, and although the family had been settled in America for nearly two hundred years, the most notable characteristics of the Caledonian race had not disappeared in him, and were transmitted in a remarkable degree of development to his illustrious son. The pertinacity of resolve, the shrewd sagacity, the practical sense, the clear judgment, the sustained energy which are conspicuous in the subject of this pamphlet, are all peculiarities that may be traced to his Scottish origin, modified of course by American influences.

The father had led an active, although not distinguished life. Born in Pennsylvania, and left an orphan at the age of eleven years, he emigrated from one State to another, and finally settled in Ohio. At the time when Ulysses was born, he dealt largely in leather, owning several tanneries. He was noted for intelligence as well as energy, and in all his dealings with men he bore an unblemished name. The mother also was a native of Pennsylvania, but had early removed to the farther West, and was married in the same State where the future general was born. Her maiden name was Simpson. The modest virtues of a Christian woman are not fit themes for public portraiture; but it is not difficult to imagine in them the source of that purity of character and almost child-like simplicity which are so singularly combined in Grant with other and apparently contradictory traits. Irving felicitously says of Washington: "Hereditary rank may be an illusion, but hereditary virtue gives a patent of nobleness beyond all the blazonry of the herald's college."

Grant was at first called Hiram Ulysses, but known always by the second name. The low-roofed cottage in which he first saw the light still overlooks the Ohio river and the opposite Kentucky shore, and his earliest hours were spent almost on the boundary line afterwards so distinctly drawn between rebellion and loyalty; in sight, indeed, of that great theatre of war on which he was to act so prominent a part. In 1823 his parents removed to Georgetown, Ohio, and there the boyhood of young Grant was passed.

Like Washington, Cromwell, Wellington, and many others whose names are world-renowned, Grant was not conspicuous in childhood beyond his fellows. Some have thought that by the reflex light of subsequent achievements they could discover in the traits of the boy the germs of all that has since appeared in the man, and doubtless those germs were all there latent, but the light and sun of circumstance had not developed them. None of his early companions saw in him any indications of his future destiny.

WEST POINT.

At the age of seventeen, an appointment to the Military Academy at West Point was offered to his father, in his behalf. The elder Grant had always been interested in politics, and the Hon. Thomas L. Hamer, with whom he had had some little misunderstanding, procured the appointment as a sort of peace-offering. Each congressional district is entitled to one representative at the Military Academy, and the youth who had been sent the year before from the district where Grant then lived failed to keep up with his class, and was dismissed in consequence. The vacancy was offered to Ulysses. Had that young predecessor been more successful, Grant might never have received a military education, or risen to distinction in arms.

On arriving at the Academy, his name was entered as Ulysses S. Grant. Mr. Hamer knew that he had a brother named Simpson, and probably confounded the two names. Grant protested against the change, but his protest did no good. He was destined to bear through life the significant initials, although they were not given him in baptism. His mates, when they discovered the blunder, with boyish perversity insisted on calling him Uncle Sam, and he finally submitted to what seemed inevitable. As Ulysses S. Grant he was commissioned in the army; as Ulysses S. Grant he is now known to his countrymen; as Ulysses S. Grant his name will live as long as the language.

Four years were spent at the Academy, but Grant made no brilliant mark there. Although a great reader, he had no fondness for study, and manifested no early aptness for his profession, except in mathematics; this science he mastered easily. Riding was his favorite accomplishment, and amusement. He was not attentive to the minutiæ of military etiquette required of the cadets, and though never guilty of serious offences and far from insubordinate, was constantly undergoing petty punishments, for having a shoe untied on parade or being late at drill. The same disregard for trivial forms has followed him through his later military career. No officer of the army to-day is less scrupulous in the etiquette of costume, or exacts from his subordinates fewer of those shows of respect which are so often paid while the reality is absent. He can indeed afford to dispense with the mere semblance of that respect which the entire army profoundly feels for his reputation and his deeds.

Among his comrades at the Academy, Grant was popular. and most of them now sincerely rejoice in his extraordinary success, although it leaves them all far behind. Some of his class, however, have risen to distinction in military and civil life. The man who graduated first was William B. Franklin, afterwards a major general of volunteers. Isaac F. Quimby also became a general officer during the rebellion, and is now a professor in a university at Rochester, New York. Among the other generals are Jos. J. Reynolds, C. C. Augur, C. S. Hamilton, Frederick Steele, Rufus Ingalls, Moses Judah, and J. J. Peck, all of whom served under their classmate during the war of the rebellion. He was twenty-first in his class at graduation, and was made a brevet second lieutenant. The army was full at the time, and its future commander could only be admitted as a supernumerary officer. He was attached to the Fourth infantry.

THE MEXICAN WAR.

At this time he was twenty-one years of age. His first post was Jefferson Barracks, near St. Louis, Missouri, where he formed the acquaintance of the lady who afterwards became his wife. She was the sister of a classmate, and the daughter of Frederick Dent, Esq., a prominent merchant of St. Louis. A few months later, the Mexican war broke out and Grant was ordered with his regiment to Texas, to join the army of General Taylor. While at Corpus Christi, he received his commission of full second lieutenant in the Seventh infantry; he had, however, become so attached to the Fourth, with which he had been serving, that a request was forwarded to Washington for permission to remain with the latter regiment; and in November, 1845, he was transferred to the Fourth infantry, in which he remained as long as he continued in the army. He was present at the battles of Palo Alto and Resaca de la Palma, and there took his first lesson in actual war; battles which must seem to him now, with his subsequent career, like insignificant skirmishes. More men have often been assigned by him to a brigade than there constituted both the American and the Mexican armies.

Lieutenant Grant remained under Taylor until the capture of Monterey, assisting in that gallant achievement. His regiment was then transferred to the army of General Scott, and participated in the siege and capture of the renowned fortress of Vera Cruz. Grant was now made quartermaster of the regiment, a position which would have honorably exempted him from exposing himself to fire, but he never allowed an opportunity of going into action to pass unimproved. He participated in the great march of Scott from the sea to the capital of Mexico, was present at all the battles of that brilliant campaign, at Chapultepec, Contreras, Churubusco, Molino del Rey, and at the capture of the City of Mexico. For his distinguished gallantry at Molino del Rey he received the brevet of first lieutenant, and in the affair which resulted in the capture of the city displayed many of the best traits which his later history has rendered so conspicuous.

A long causeway led up from the mountain of Chapultepec to one of the gates of the city of Mexico, but was so well defended that it was judged more feasible to approach it by an indirect route. Worth's division accordingly was sent by a road which entered the city from the west; Grant was in Worth's division.

An abrupt turn in the road was defended by a parapet, with a single embrasure, and as the advance, of which Grant was one, approached this parapet, a raking fire of musketry made it necessary for the assailants to avail themselves of every chance for cover. Grant, however, went alone across the space exposed to fire, and discovered an opportunity to flank the parapet. Hastening back to his men, some twenty or thirty in number, he called out that he had found a chance to turn the enemy's position, and asked for volunteers. Ten or a dozen soldiers jumped up at once, and were soon crawling with him behind a stone fence, towards the place from which they were to storm the little work; when Grant discovered Captain, now General, Horace Brooks coming up in the same direction with a company. Brooks was a cautious soldier, and, making his way slowly along in the bottom of a ditch; Grant at once cried out, "Captain, I've found a way to flank the enemy;" and Brooks replied, "Well, you know the route, go on and we will follow." So the lieutenant led, and the whole party, now nearly fifty in number, assaulted the end of the parapet, carried it by storm, and then took the enemy in rear. The Mexicans fled at once from the position, no longer tenable, and the parapet was secured.

The party was now on the direct road to the Garita San Cosme, one of the strongest entrances to the city of Mexico, whose spires were distinctly visible. On they went, till they found their way obstructed by another parapet, exactly like that already carried, but this one defended by a cannon. Grant again advanced at the head of his little column, by this time augmented to a hundred and fifty soldiers, and the second parapet was carried. But they were at last under the guns of the city itself, and Brooks, who assumed command by virtue of seniority, declared that he could not hold the position long without reinforcements. Grant was therefore sent back to General Worth to ask for more troops. He had not been gone five minutes before the little command was driven pell-mell from the parapet. He, however, soon found the commanding general, and fresh troops were at once sent forward.

A little to the right of the parapet, but still nearer to the garita, was a church, with a steeple nearly a hundred feet high. Grant promptly led a section of artillery towards the church through the ditches with which the whole country is broken. He found the padre, and demanded the keys of the sacred building, which the father was at first unwilling to surrender, but Grant soon convinced him of the necessity of compliance. The mountain howitzer, drawn by hand, was speedily taken to pieces, and four or five men carried it to the belfry. Grant disposed the rest of the force around the church below so as to secure it against easy capture, and mounted the steeple. The pieces of the howitzer were hastily put together, and Grant himself pointed and served the gun, which quickly drove the enemy from the parapet. The piece was then directed on the city, and did excellent execution against the garita. The confusion of the Mexicans, who hastened to retreat inside the city, was plainly visible.

Worth soon perceived the shells issuing from this novel position, and marked the effect they were doing on the enemy. He was delighted at the sagacity and gallantry of the performance, and sent at once for Grant to congratulate him. Not only did he do this publicly, but he placed a captain, with an entire company, under Grant's command, and bade him return with another howitzer to his church. Grant obeyed, and that night the Garita San Cosmo surrendered. On the morrow Mexico was in the hands of the Americans.

For this achievement, so important and so successful, which was executed without orders by a second lieutenant, acting as a quartermaster, who therefore had no legitimate command, but was obliged to gather up men and weapons on the field, Grant was mentioned in all the official reports, and received another brevet five days after the former. One of his fellow second lieutenants in the fourth infantry at this time, was named Abram Lincoln. He died in Florida, in 1852. Generals McCall, Alvord, Prince, Augur, Judah, Hays, and Russell, were also among his comrades, most of them then of higher rank than he who has since outstripped them all.

PANAMA.

After the close of the Mexican war, Grant returned with his regiment to the United States. He married in April, 1848, and for a while was in command of his company, first at Detroit, and afterwards at Sackett's Harbor. In 1851 he was ordered to Oregon by way of California. His wife was left behind. The route was by sea to the Isthmus of Panama, but in crossing the isthmus the cholera broke out among the passengers.

Grant was again acting as quartermaster. The railroad at this time was completed only about thirty miles; after that the route was in boats up the Chagres river, to the head of navigation, and from this point about thirty miles farther by land. The troops, some seven hundred in number, were to march from the river to the Pacific, but the steamship company had contracted to furnish mules and other transportation for the sick, as well as for the wives and children of the officers and soldiers. There were, however, several hundred other passengers besides the soldiers, and when the cholera appeared the panic among them was great. The passengers offered higher prices to the natives than the company had bargained to pay, and the Indians hired to them all their mules and wagons, leaving none for the soldiers or their families. The great body of troops at once marched on, but Grant was left with the sick and the women and children, who were unable to walk under the July sun of the tropics. Here he remained a week, amid malignant heats and pestilence and death, taking entire command of everything, making extraordinary efforts to procure transportation, caring for the sick and dying, burying the dead, controlling the half-hostile natives, and doing the work of a dozen frightened officers. During all this week he never took his clothes off once, and only snatched rare intervals of sleep as he lay stretched along a bench or under a shed, exposed to the miasma of the forest and the swamps. But he was preserved for still greater emergencies. Neither Mexican bullets nor South American plagues were allowed to harm the life destined thereafter to be of so much consequence to his countrymen.

Finally, as the agents of the steamship failed entirely to do their duty, Grant took upon himself the responsibility of making a new contract in their name. He hired mules and wagons and litters for the sick at prices double those which the company had agreed to pay. He engaged natives to bury the dead, and at last took up his march for the Pacific. About a hundred and fifty souls had been left with him in the interior of the isthmus, half of whom perished in that week of cholera. Grant was among the last to start from the fatal spot, from which many officers in his situation would not have scrupled to flee at the first appearance of the pestilence.

CIVIL LIFE.

His regiment finally arrived at Fort Dallas, Oregon, and in 1853 he received his commission of captain. He remained on the Pacific coast till 1854, when, having served in the army eleven years, he resigned his commission and returned to St. Louis. Near this place he owned a little farm. His means were limited, and he was accustomed to work at the plough with his hired men, and one or two slaves, the property of his wife. In the winter, when the cultivation of the ground was impossible, he resorted to wood-cutting, cutting and cording the wood himself, and hauling it to market in St. Louis, a distance of eleven miles. His dress and appearance were that of a sturdy woodman. He built a log-house on his farm, and lived simply, spending most of his time with his family, for his habits were domestic. He was never so happy as when with his wife and children. He now had three sons and a daughter.

Once in a while, on driving his cart into town, he met some old army friends who were stationed at his former post of Jefferson Barracks. These were always glad to welcome him and talk over other times, thinking it no disgrace to him that he endeavored to earn an honest livelihood, though in a plain and humble way. Yet some of his other and more fashionable associates sometimes turned their heads if they saw him approaching in a woodman's blouse. The same men since have been conspicuous in asking favors of him whom they once were unwilling to recognize.

But with all his industry he did not succeed. He tried collecting money, but for this he had no talent. He was too modest to thrive at the dunning trade, and at times his circumstances were narrow indeed. Providence was preparing him, by hardships and experiences of every sort, to know both himself and the people whose destinies he was thereafter to guide. Had he been luxuriously bred, the traits which adverse fortune developed might have been smothered in the hot-bed of success; the endurance, the patience, the knowledge of men, the persistency of purpose which stood this nation in so much stead in her hour of peril, might never have ripened to their fruition in the last eight years.

In 1859, finding that he made no progress in St. Louis, Grant removed with his family to Galena, where his father and brothers were engaged in the leather trade. They gave him occupation, and here he remained nearly a year. His house was simple, like his habits; his daily employment was trading leather, at wholesale and retail. He seemed to have forgotten his military life and pursuits. The title of captain, by which he still was known, hardly recalled to him the storming of Chapultepec or the guns that he so gallantly mounted in crazy steeples under the walls of Mexico. There was no indication visible to any of the inhabitants of Galena which foretold that he should ever become the foremost man in America. No restless ambition disturbed his spirits, no craving for fame made him dissatisfied with obscurity. Those nearest him never suspected that he possessed extraordinary ability. He himself never dreamed that he was destined to great place and power. Like Washington and Cromwell, he lived far retired from the haunts of public men, until the needs of his time and his country called him forth.

Yet all this while he was known for practical sense, for good clear judgment, for moderate but determined opinions, for scrupulous purity, for staunch friendships, for all the traits that make up the character of a man of honor. All this while he made men love him who knew him well, and saw him so free from guile, so full of warm affection.

All this while, unconscious to himself, he was laying the foundations of that greatness which to-day is known in both hemispheres. This varied experience of soldier, farmer, and trader, of northern and southern, of eastern and western life, this frontier career, these two years in a foreign land, this dealing with the people of Oregon and Michigan, of New York and St. Louis and Galena, gave him a wide and thorough sympathy with all classes of the American people; made him, unknown to himself, a representative American. In war, he had served under the two greatest captains that the American army had produced during the century; he had seen the strategy of Taylor and Scott, he had shared in the battles of each, had witnessed marches and sieges and assaults. In peace, the leather merchant of Galena, now thirty-nine years old, had seen and learned more of life, had laid its lessons more to heart than many of his countrymen whose names were then well known to fame.

He had learned patience when hope was long deferred; he had learned courage and endurance under heavy and repeated difficulties; he had shown that he possessed persistency of resolve and fertility of resource; that he never despaired. If one means failed he tried another. He had shown, above all, content under ill fortur e and with little things, and was now ready, though he dreamed not of it, for great achievements and extraordinary place and power. Until the country had need of him, Providence kept him in training for the emergencies with which he was to cope. But now the fullness of time had arrived.

OUTBREAK OF THE WAR.

The abolition or extension of slavery was a question which had agitated the American Union ever since that Union had existed. A majority of the inhabitants of the South were determined that the institution should be extended into all the territory not already divided into States. A majority of the population of the North was equally determined that it should be restrained within the limits of those States where it already existed.

The Republican party was inaugurated for the express purpose of preventing the extension of slavery, and finally succeeded in obtain-ing possession of the Government. Upon this event the leaders of the South at once determined on forcible resistance. They indeed had long meant to sever all connection with the North, and set up an independent government for themselves, but hitherto had been obliged to veil their intentions. Now, however, they succeeded in dragging the entire population of the South after them and with them into rebellion. An armed attack was made upon a national fort in the harbor of Charleston, South Carolina. The forces of the Government resisted, but the rebels were successful, and Fort Sumter submitted to what was called the Confederacy. From this moment the great mass of the people at the North forgot all their old political differences, and set themselves about the work of suppressing the revolt. A few traitors lingered here and there, but they dared not openly give utterance to their sentiments, and were lost in the mighty uprising of the nation determined to protect its own existence. The South, on the contrary, was all swept into the vortex of treason, and the mightiest civil war in history was inaugurated.

Two days after the outbreak of the war, the President issued a call for seventy-five thousand volunteer troops, and three days after that proclamation appeared, a public meeting was held in Galena, in response to the call; Captain Grant presided. He had never occupied a position of this character before; he was no politician, but his former connection with the regular army gave him a fitness for the post, and, although he had voted for Buchanan against Frémont, in 1856, he was untainted with any secession doctrine. The attack upon the flag under which he had fought appealed to every instinct of his nature, every principle of his intellect, and he immediately determined that his place was in the field. He had been educated by the country, and felt that the country had an especial right to his services in her hour of trial. He at once began to put his affairs in order, and in less than a week was drilling a company of volunteers. On the 23d of April he started with his company for Springfield, the capital of Illinois. His services were then offered to the Governor of the State, who at this period, when the simplest principles of military organization were unfamiliar, was glad to avail himself of the knowledge of an old army officer. Grant served five weeks, most of the time mustering in new troops, under the direction of the Governor. Meanwhile, he wrote to Washington, and offered himself to the National Government in any capacity that might be desired. His letter, however, was not answered, it was not even put on file, and the insignificant captain received no reply. This, however, did not repel him from the duty which he owed his country, and he went to Cincinnati, hoping to obtain a position on the staff of Major General McClellan. He was too modest to make an application, and nothing was offered him.

He did not even succeed in gaining access to McClellan's presence. Still, he was resolved to enter the army, and returned to his mustering at Springfield, where, early in June, he was offered the twenty-first regiment of Illinois volunteers. It was a fortunate day for the country when Governor Yates made out the commission for the man who was fated to lead the American armies to so many victories.

Colonel Grant at once took command of his regiment, and was stationed at first in Missouri, where he was occupied in watching the movements of various guerrilla bands, by which that State was infested. Shortly afterwards the Hon. E. B. Washburne suggested his name to the President for a brigadier generalship. Mr. Washburne had long been the member of Congress from Galena, but first made Grant's acquaintance at the public meeting held there after the President's first call for troops. He then noticed the fervid patriotism and prompt energy of the captain, and, seeing him again at Springfield, was again impressed with his diligence and earnestness in a subordinate position, and, when the President asked who should be appointed a brigadier from Illinois, Washburne suggested Colonel Grant. On the 7th of August the new general was commissioned, to date from May 17. He knew nothing of his promotion for some time afterwards, till a friend called his attention to the announcement in the newspapers. Washburne had never spoken nor written to him on the subject, and his surprise was great to find himself a brigadier. No promotion indeed that he ever received was suggested or procured or expedited by any act or word of his. All his honors have come to him unsought.

PADUCAH.

On the 1st of September, 1861, General Frémont, his immediate commander, created for him the district of southeast Missouri, with headquarters at Cairo, Illinois. His duty was to protect the country near the junction of the Ohio, Mississippi, Tennessee, and Kentucky rivers. None of this region had then been formally occupied by rebel troops; and even the national forces had not entered the State of Kentucky, which at that time claimed to be neutral in the contest. But it was evident that this neutrality would not long be respected by the rebel authorities; neither was it recognized by those who fought for the Union. Two days after Grant arrived at Cairo, he heard that the rebel General Polk had invaded the State, seizing two important places on the Mississippi, and threatening Paducah at the point where the Tennessee river empties into the Ohio. This latter place it was important to secure, as it commanded the navigation of both streams. Grant at once informed Frémont of the news, adding, "I am getting ready to go to Paducah. Will start at six-and-a-half o'clock." That night he did start, having received no orders from Frémont. He embarked two regiments and a battery on transports, and, steaming up the Ohio, arrived at Paducah next morning, seized the town without firing a gun, and secured this important place, which never afterwards passed out of the national possession. A rebel general officer and his staff were in the town, making preparations for its occupancy, but escaped by the railroad while the national troops were landing, and a large rebel force was only sixteen miles off; but Kentucky, by this bold stroke, was secured to the Union. The Legislature at once declared in favor of the Government, and all talk of the secession or neutrality of the State was abandoned. Kentucky was, indeed, a battle-ground long and often afterwards, but its authorities from that time were firm in their allegiance. Grant himself went back the same day to Cairo, and found there Frémont's permission to take Paducah, "if he felt strong enough."

BELMONT.

Nothing of importance occurred after this for nearly eight weeks. Troops were added to Grant's command, and all his time was spent in drilling and organizing them. They were of course entirely raw, officers and men were ignorant of the very rudiments of the military art; and Grant never worked harder in his life than in preparing these new soldiers to take the field. Early in November he got orders from Frémont to make a demonstration upon a little place called Belmont, on the west bank of the Mississippi, some twenty miles below Cairo. It had no importance in itself, for it was directly under the guns of Columbus, a considerable work on the opposite shore. Columbus was too strongly fortified and too largely garrisoned to allow any chance of its capture, but rebel forces were being sent from there into Missouri, and annoying Frémont's operations in that State. Grant was accordingly instructed to move troops south from Cairo, on both sides of the river, with a view to distract the enemy and prevent any further crossing. The day after this order was given, however, Frémont sent word of a rebel force in Missouri, about fifty miles to the southwest of Cairo, and ordered Grant to intercept it. Accordingly, on the 3d of November, Grant sent three thousand men, under Colonel Oglesby, in the direction indicated. This delayed the demonstration previously contemplated. But on the 5th Frémont again telegraphed that reinforcements were being sent from Columbus, and directed the original demonstration to be made at once. In obedience to this, Grant the same day despatched several regiments to the rear of Columbus, with orders not to attack, but to keep the enemy from throwing more force across the river, and on the 6th he moved himself, with three thousand men on transports, down the river towards Belmont. During the night he learned that still larger forces had been sent by the rebels from Columbus, to interrupt the troops that he had ordered into Missouri three days before. This decided him to make an absolute attack on Belmont, in order to bring back the rebels from the interior of Missouri, and thus save the detachment under Oglesby. He determined to destroy or capture all the troops at Belmont, and get off again before the rebels could reinforce.

Landing at daybreak about three miles above Belmont, he marched at once in the direction of the rebel camp. But the enemy soon came out to meet him, and a desperate encounter ensued, lasting several hours, during which Grant was in the thickest of the fight, and had his horse shot under him. He finally drove the rebels in great confusion to their camp, which was defended by a rough abatis. This, however, proved insufficient to stay the soldiers of the Union, and the rebels fled in dismay to the river bank, where they were covered by the guns of their great fort at Columbus. Grant having accomplished his object, now strove to get his men together and return, but the confusion consequent upon victory was too much for these raw troops. They shouted and ran around the camps, and were utterly uncontrollable. The rebels meanwhile had begun to send reinforcements across the river from Columbus, and it was necessary to do something at once. Accordingly, Grant ordered his staff officers to set the camps on fire, and then the men returned to the ranks. They were marching back in good order to their boats when the rebel reinforcements arrived, and, making a short cut, threw themselves directly in front of Grant's little column. The national soldiers were at first greatly disturbed at the sight, supposing themselves cut off. One of Grant's officers came up to him in dismay with the news that they were surrounded. But Grant remarked, calmly, "If that is so, *we must cut our way out as we cut our way in.*" The troops at once took heart, when they found they had a leader, and Grant calling out, "*We have whipped them once, I think we can do it again,"* they rallied, charged, and again dispersed the enemy, who retreated once more under cover of the river banks.

The rebel reinforcements, however, continued to arrive in great numbers, and Grant pushed his men on rapidly, but remained himself farther behind, to superintend those who were gathering up the wounded. While thus engaged he got entirely outside of his own soldiers, and directly in front of the third rebel line, which was now greatly increased and advancing rapidly towards the national transports. Grant fortunately wore a private's overcoat, for the day was cold, and the rebels did not recognize him for an officer. A rebel general, indeed, cried out, "There, men, is a Yankee, if you want to try your aim," but they were too eager to reach the steamers then, and nobody aimed at Grant. He, however, saw that there was no time to lose, and, putting spurs to his horse, rode rapidly back to his command.

By this time the enemy had opened a heavy musketry fire, and Grant got aboard under a storm of bullets. His men were already on the transports before him, and at once put off. The rebels fired too high, and no one was killed, while two gunboats that had acted as a convoy for the troops opened with grape and canister, and did great execution in the enemy's ranks. Seven thousand rebels were engaged in this fight against Grant's three thousand, and the enemy lost six hundred men, a third more than Grant. Grant carried off two pieces of artillery, and nearly two hundred prisoners.

This was the first battle in which he commanded, and it illustrated in a peculiar degree the coolness and judgment and gallantry for which he afterwards was so remarkable. The promptness with which he decided upon converting the demonstration into an attack, the vigor of his movement, the equanimity with which he sustained the spirits of his troops when they flagged under unexpected appearances of reverse, and the steadiness with which he acted when greatly outnumbered, were all traits that foretold to those who could read them, the ability of a great commander.

FORT HENRY

Two days after the battle of Belmont, General Frémont was superseded by General Halleck, who made no immediate change in Grant's command. The rebels at this time were in great strength at Columbus, holding the Mississippi river from that place downward. A line drawn eastward from the Father of Waters at Columbus, would strike the Tennessee and Cumberland rivers a few miles north of the boundary between Kentucky and Tennessee. Near this boundary two forts were erected, one on each stream; that on the Tennessee was called Fort Henry, that on the Cumberland, Fort Donelson. Still further east, at Bowling Green, about a hundred and twenty miles from the Mississippi, another great depot of men and arms was established by the enemy.

These various points constituted an admirable line, stretching nearly across the State of Kentucky, behind which rebellion was rampant and secure, and beyond which it constantly threatened to sally against the forces of the Government. Grant early conceived the idea of piercing this line at its centre, by the capture of Fort Henry. He proposed this in conversation with Halleck in January, 1862, but received a rebuff for his pains. Notwithstanding, on the 28th of the same month, he repeated the proposition by telegraph; "*With permission, I will take and hold Fort Henry*, on the Tennessee, and establish and hold a large camp there." The next day he wrote at length, detailing the advantages of the movement, and insisting on the necessity of prompt action, before the rebel defenses should be so strengthened as to become impregnable. In this application he was joined by Commodore Foote, who commanded the naval force in the western waters, but was under Halleck's orders. Halleck now consented to the movement, and on the next day, February 2d, Grant started from Cairo with seventeen hundred men on transports. Foote accompanied him with seven gunboats. They reached a point on the Tennessee three miles below Fort Henry on the 4th, and the troops at once began to land. Fort Henry was on the eastern shore, and a small but unfinished work was on the opposite bank. The two places were garrisoned by two thousand eight hundred men, under General Tilghman. The Tennessee and the Cumberland rivers are at this point only twelve miles apart, and a direct road connected Fort Henry with Fort Donelson.

Grant's plan was to surround Fort Henry on the land side with his troops, so as to cut off the garrison either from reinforcements or from any chance of escape, while Foote was to attack in front with his gunboats. The Tennessee, however, had overflowed its banks, so that the roads were almost impassable. Bridges were swept away, and the rain was falling in torrents. Besides this, Grant had not

2

steamers enough to bring all his troops from Cairo at once, and, having debarked a portion, was obliged to send back his transports for the remainder. This delayed his movements a day or two, and the rebels availed themselves of the chance to strengthen the fort. It was not until near midnight of the 5th that all of Grant's troops could be got ashore.

The landing was north of the fort, and just outside of the range of its guns. Two brigades were ordered to disembark on the western bank, and seize the opposite work, while the remainder were to march at eleven o'clock on the morning of the 6th, and take position east of Fort Henry, so as to invest it, and "be ready to charge and take the work by storm promptly on the receipt of orders." These instructions were given out before all the troops had arrived, but it was reported that the rebels were reinforcing, and it was therefore necessary to be prompt.

The troops moved at the hour appointed, but they had eight miles to march, streams to bridge, and roads to cut through the woods, the ordinary ones having been destroyed by the freshet. Meanwhile Foote advanced and attacked with his gunboats, and in less than an hour and a half the fort surrendered. Only sixty men, however, were captured, for Tilghman, the rebel commander, foreseeing the probability of not being able to hold out, had stationed the rest of the garrison, over two thousand seven hundred strong, at the outworks, about two miles off, and before the fight began he sent them orders to retreat upon Fort Donelson. They obeyed, and, when Grant got up from struggling through the swamps and mire, the main rebel force had escaped. The fort, with seventeen heavy guns, was turned over to him by Foote, and a detachment of cavalry was sent out at once to pursue the retreating enemy. The rebels, however, had already got too far for this to avail; a few prisoners and two guns were captured, and the pursuit was abandoned.

FORT DONELSON.

The same day Grant telegraphed to Halleck, "Fort Henry is ours." He gave, however, the credit where it was due: "The gunboats silenced the batteries before the investment was completed." Then, with the same almost laughable audacity with which he had announced that "with permission he would take and hold Fort Henry," he added, "*I shall take and destroy Fort Donelson on the 8th, and return to Fort*

Henry." At this time Halleck had never mentioned the subject of Fort Donelson to Grant, but the latter, with the clear perception and quick decision which are so indispensable in a great soldier, at once saw the necessity of acting before the rebels had recovered from the effect of the blow already dealt. He therefore determined *without orders.* The roads, however, again impeded his movements. The whole country was inundated, and Fort Henry almost an island. The troops had to be used for a day or two in saving what had been gained from the rapidly-rising deluge. Meanwhile Halleck forwarded reinforcements. He gave, however, no encouragement to Grant's advance. He countermanded nothing, it is true, but all his despatches dwelt on the necessity of defending Fort Henry, while all of Grant's idea was to attack Fort Donelson. That, he thought, was the surest way to defend Fort Henry. While one was telegraphing about picks and shovels on the Tennessee, the other replied by asking for heavy ordnance for the siege on the Cumberland.

The rebels now were wide awake to their danger, and, hurrying troops to Fort Donelson ; they also strained every nerve to strengthen its defence on all sides, and succeeded in making one of the most formidable works that had been constructed at that period of the war. Grant was ready to start by the 10th, but Foote had sent some of his gunboats up the river, and it was necessary to wait for their return. On the 11th, however, Foote started with the fleet and all the reinforcements that had yet arrived from Halleck. These went around by the Ohio and Cumberland rivers, and the same day Grant's advance moved out in the rear of Fort Henry, three or four miles towards Fort Donelson. On the 12th the main column, fifteen thousand strong, was in motion. The orders were to take *neither tents nor baggage, but forty rounds of ammunition per man.* No rations were furnished, except those in haversacks, as supplies were to meet them on their arrival at the Cumberland. Before noon they came in sight of the enemy's lines.

The fort itself was on an eminence commanding the Cumberland, and covered over a hundred acres. It was manned by seventeen heavy guns. Outside of this were two strong lines of entrenchments with abatis. These lines were admirably located on commanding ridges, and protected by detached works ; the nature of the ground also afforded a peculiar defence to the rebels, broken as it was by ravines and streams and rugged hills. On each side of the rebel line was a creek, whose waters were now high, and these creeks furnished additional defences to the besieged, whose line was nearly three miles long, stretching from stream to stream. The garrison, nearly twenty-two thousand strong, was commanded by General Floyd, the traitorous member of Buchanan's Cabinet, whose perfidy in civil life was destined to be eclipsed by the baseness with which he deserted his fellow rebels when disaster became inevitable.

Thus, with his little army, not more than two-thirds as large as the rebel force, and with one or two light batteries, Grant marched up to a formidable work, defended by heavy artillery and sixty-seven field guns, *as daring an attempt as is presented in the history of war.* As yet no reinforcements had arrived, and the gunboats had not appeared. Halleck thought his subordinate was still fortifying Fort Henry, but Grant was convinced that unless this movement were made with promptness, Fort Donelson would not be taken at all, and he had confidence in himself and in his men. The investment was begun at once, and by nightfall the Union left rested on the creek north of the fort, while the right reached nearly to the stream on the south. All the next day was spent in studying the ground and perfecting the investment, but the attack could not begin, as neither the reinforcements nor the gunboats had arrived. The aspect of affairs was gloomy. The besieging force, unsupported, uncovered by works, and in front of an army so much larger than itself, was in imminent peril. Two or three engagements occurred along the lines, provoked without Grant's orders, and the result of these was not encouraging. But the enemy, fortunately, did not come out in force.

All night the cold was intense. It was February, and the ground was covered with snow. Hail fell fast, and a more inclement storm was never known in that latitude. The troops were without tents; many were frozen, their rations were scanty, and the pickets were so close to the enemy that no camp-fires could be allowed. An interchange of shots continued all night, and the groans of the wounded were mingled with the shrieking of the wind, the whistling of bullets, and the crash of falling trees, cut down either by the storm or the fire of the enemy. Before daylight, however, Foote arrived with the reinforcements and supplies—a welcome sight, indeed. The garrison left at Fort Henry had also been ordered across by land, leaving only a small force there. Grant's command now consisted of three divisions; McClernand had the right, Lewis Wallace the centre, and C. F. Smith the left of his line.

At three o'clock on the afternoon of the 14th, Foote attacked the

fort with six gunboats. Grant's forces were all under arms, ready to
assault on the land side, in case of success in the water attack. But
Foote was unfortunate; two of his vessels were entirely disabled, and
two others rendered temporarily unmanageable. He himself was
wounded and obliged to withdraw. That night he requested Grant
to come aboard his flagship, and there declared that his fleet was so
much damaged as to render it necessary for him to return to Cairo
for repairs. He urged Grant not to attack in his absence, and this
indeed seemed the truest policy for the national general. It was not,
however, the policy of the enemy to allow such a course. Grant's
reinforcements were pouring in fast; his army was now equal in
numbers to the besieged, though in artillery, and of course in position it was still far inferior. While Grant was on the flagship, consulting with Foote, the rebels, too, held a council of war. They perceived that if they remained quiet they would certainly be completely
surrounded, and eventually compelled to surrender. They determined, therefore, to mass on their left, and, coming out of their lines
on the morning of the 15th, assault Grant's right, which was his
weakest wing, not quite extending to the creek on the south side of
the fort.

They acted promptly, and at early dawn assaulted McClernand in
great numbers. The national defence was vigorous, but vain, and
McClernand was pushed back upon the centre. Lewis Wallace supported him with nearly all his force, and the battle raged heavily here
for hours. The rebels maintained the fight with artillery as well as
infantry, and in numbers decidedly superior to those engaged against
them. Grant meanwhile was on the gunboat, which he did not leave
till morning, as his interview with Foote was important and protracted.
No noise of the conflict had reached his ears, for the wind blew in an
opposite direction, and the fight was on the extreme southern point of
the entire position, while the fleet had of course withdrawn to the
north.

It was nine o'clock before Grant got ashore. As he was approaching his headquarters, he was met with news of the battle still raging.
He at once directed Smith, whose troops had not been engaged, to get
himself in readiness to attack, as this would be the quickest way to
relieve the hard-pressed forces on the right. Then riding on, he
speedily arrived at that part of the field where the fighting had been
most severe. The rebels had not succeeded in forcing their way
through, and were slowly finding a route back towards their works.

The national troops had held their ground, but were very much disordered; in no condition to follow up the enemy. They were mostly raw, and had been taken aback by the rebel assault; especially the news that the enemy had come out with knapsacks and haversacks seemed to appal them. They told this to Grant as evidence that the rebels meant to stay outside of their works and fight for several days. He, however, at once detected the significance of this news. "Are the haversacks filled?" he asked. Prisoners were examined, and the haversacks found to contain three days' rations. "Then they mean to cut their way out; they have no idea of staying here to fight us." He saw immediately why the haversacks were filled. The plan of the rebels to break through the investment and escape was evident to him at a glance. It was also evident that if they made this plan they must be despairing, and now, therefore, was the time to attack them.

He looked around the field, and saw both sides exhausted; either was ready to retreat if hard pressed. This was the moment to convert battle into victory. "*Whichever party first attacks now will win*," he exclaimed, "*and the rebels will have to be very quick if they beat me.*" He set his staff to work to reassure the drooping spirits of the soldiers. He told the troops himself that the attack of the morning was the last desperate effort of the enemy to escape. He revived their confidence and inspired their courage. The men had been disorganized and scattered all over the field, but they took new heart at this idea, and returned at once to the ranks. Then he rode rapidly back to the left, and ordered Smith to attack immediately and with all his force, while the other two divisions which had been so hotly engaged all day were to take advantage of this diversion of Smith, and recover the advantage they had almost lost.

Smith advanced at once and with great alacrity. The ground was exceedingly difficult, but he charged at the head of his troops, and the effect was irresistible. He carried everything before him, penetrated the first line of entrenchments, and secured a hill which commanded all within; in fact, the key to the possession of the fort. The troops on the right advanced at the same time, and as the enemy was obliged to hurry to the defence of the point in front of Smith, Wallace and McClernand regained their ground and the guns they had lost in the morning. It was dark before the battle ceased, and only darkness saved the rebels from losing their entire fort by storm. Still it was evident to both sides that the place was won.

At daylight next morning, a white flag was sent to Grant with propositions for surrender. Floyd had deserted his command; Pillow, the next in rank, had followed his example, and General S. B. Buckner was left at the head of the rebel force. He asked for an armistice, and the appointment of commissioners to settle terms of capitulation. Grant, who was preparing to storm the works, appreciated thoroughly the situation of affairs, and replied in the well-known words: *"No terms except unconditional and immediate surrender can be accepted. I propose to move immediately upon your works."* Buckner had no option and at once acquiesced. Grant, however, allowed the officers to retain their swords, and both officers and men their personal effects. He had no desire unnecessarily to humiliate those whom he had captured. The same spirit which he displayed then was manifest again and again during the war. *It was his lot to receive the surrender of more and larger forces than any other soldier of modern times.* He was always as unconditional and determined in battle as at Donelson, and always as magnanimous in victory, again and again extracting from the very men whom he conquered, tributes of gratitude. Buckner in this instance took Grant with him to his troops, and told them of the kindness and consideration with which the rebel army had been treated by their victor.

Grant captured at this place *fifteen thousand men, seventeen thousand muskets, and sixty-five pieces of artillery.* The rebels had lost two thousand five hundred in killed and wounded, and nearly four thousand escaped in steamers in the night up the river, or made their way on horses through the swollen creek on the south of Fort Donelson. Grant's force at the time of the surrender amounted to twenty-seven thousand; but his reinforcements were constantly coming up for several days afterwards. His losses during the siege were four hundred and twenty-five killed, and one thousand five hundred and sixteen wounded and missing. The results of this achievement extended, however, far beyond the capture of men and material. The Tennessee and Cumberland rivers were now opened to the national forces, and two great highways unbarred, by which access to the interior of the rebellious region was made secure. The entire States of Tennessee and Kentucky were uncovered. Nashville, the capital of Tennessee, surrendered to the troops of Buell, for it was now defenceless. Fort Donelson had been its bulwark. Columbus, on the Mississippi, and Bowling Green, a hundred miles to the east, where the rebels had collected one of their largest armies, were turned, and both speedily evacuated. The country rang with applause. Grant was made a major general of volunteers, and from this time his name has been familiar in every household in America.

Up to the capture of Fort Donelson no very brilliant or decided success had attended the national arms. Other commanders had promised much; much had been expected from them; but nothing had been accomplished. Suddenly this obscure soldier in the West, whose very name was unknown to nine-tenths of his countrymen, achieved a victory that lifted up the national heart, that inspirited the army, that displayed ability of the highest military order, and promised further success wherever he should command. From the extreme of depression to an elation almost without parallel, the people passed at one bound. Had they known then, how often again this same commander was destined, in an hour of sadness and defeat, to lead their armies to brilliant victory, and crown their hopes with more than fruition, their gratitude would have been as boundless as his services were destined to be unparalleled.

SHILOH.

Donelson fell on the 16th of February, 1862, and on the 1st of March, Grant was ordered to move his entire column up the Tennessee river, as far as Eastport, Mississippi, in order to destroy the railroad connections at Corinth, Jackson, and Humboldt. These orders reached him on the 2d of March, and on the 4th his army was in motion. The same day Halleck telegraphed him to turn over the command to C. F. Smith, one of his subordinates, and remain himself at Fort Henry. This was in consequence of some statements made to Halleck, that Grant had neglected his duty at Fort Donelson, and overstepped it in other instances, going to Nashville without leave. Halleck immediately telegraphed news of these acts to McClellan, then general-in-chief at Washington, and received permission not only to relieve Grant from duty, but to place him in arrest. A long and animated correspondence ensued, the upshot of which was that Halleck withdrew all his accusations, declaring to the Government that Grant had acted entirely from praiseworthy motives, and that all the reported irregularities had been satisfactorily explained. He also wrote flattering letters to Grant, and restored him to his command, but failed to inform him that the trouble had originated in his own reports to Washington.

On the 13th of March, Grant was ordered to resume his command,

and on the 17th rejoined his troops. He wrote to Sherman on that day, "I have just arrived, and although sick for the last few weeks, *begin to feel better at the thought of being again with the troops.*" The expedition under Smith had accomplished nothing, and the army was now divided, a part being at Pittsburg Landing, on the western bank of the Tennessee, and the remainder at Savanna, a point on the opposite shore, about nine miles lower down. The bulk of the troops were at Pittsburg Landing, from which they threatened Corinth, the junction of two great southern railroads, one running from Memphis to Charleston, the other from Mobile to the Ohio river. These roads connected the most distant extremities of the rebellious region, and it was of the highest importance to the enemy to protect them, and to the Government to obtain possession of them. The rebels accordingly, after their crushing defeat at Donelson, and the abandonment of their first great line, collected a large force at Corinth, to resist there any farther advance of Grant. Both parties bent all their efforts to secure this point. Halleck was given command of all the forces in Kentucky and Tennessee, as well as those in Missouri, and sent large reinforcements to Grant, besides ordering Buell's entire army, forty thousand strong, to move from Nashville to Grant's support.

As soon as Grant arrived at his post, he removed all his troops to the western side of the river, at Pittsburg Landing, but remained himself for a few days at Savanna, where he could more easily superintend the organization of his daily arriving forces, and also communicate more directly with Buell, now on his way from Nashville. By the 20th of March, Buell was at Columbia, but from that point the roads were bad and his movements slow, and it took him seventeen days to get to Savanna. Meanwhile, Grant had distributed his troops into six divisions, under Generals McClernand, Smith, Wallace, Sherman, Hurlbut, and Prentiss. He was about removing his headquarters to the eastern bank of the Tennessee, when he received a message from Buell, dated the 4th of April, stating that he would arrive on the 5th, and requesting Grant to remain at Savanna to meet him. With this Grant complied. Every day, however, he visited the front, at Pittsburg Landing.

On the fourth, a serious skirmish took place between some of Sherman's troops and a body of the enemy, now known to be in large force at Corinth, nineteen miles from the Landing. Grant rode out to the front with Sherman after this, and they both agreed that no probability of an immediate battle existed. Still Grant thought it best to be on the alert, and made various dispositions of troops, so as to be prepared in case of an important emergency. He instructed division commanders to hold themselves in readiness to support each other if attacked, and directed a sharp lookout to be kept with the advance guards. The pickets of several divisions were doubled in consequence, and cavalry patrols pushed out a mile and a half. On the 5th of April, the advance division of Buell's army arrived at Savanna, under General Nelson, and was ordered by Grant to be in readiness to reinforce the troops on the west bank.

Meanwhile the rebel army, over forty thousand strong, under Albert Sidney Johnson, had marched from Corinth, on the 3d of April, intending to attack Grant before Buell could arrive. The roads, however, were bad, and Johnson was not ready to assault before the 6th, which was Sunday. Grant's troops were now disposed in two lines, the first about three miles out from the Tennessee. Two creeks emptying into the Tennessee, formed the right and left defences of his army. That on the right was known as Owl creek, that on the left was called Lick creek. Sherman's division was most advanced on the extreme right, near a meeting house called Shiloh Chapel; to his left, but somewhat in the rear, was McClernand, then Prentiss, and on the extreme left a detached brigade of Sherman's division. The second line, a mile or more in rear, was composed of Smith's division on the right, this day commanded by W. H. L. Wallace, because of Smith's illness, and Hurlbut on the left. Lewis Wallace's division was at Crump's Landing, about five miles to the right of Sherman, covering an important road, by which the whole Union army might otherwise have been turned. The two lines faced south and southwest. There were no entrenchments. At this time, troops on neither side were accustomed to protect themselves in the open field, but the two streams upon which the army rested were both flooded, and the banks of Lick creek, on the left, were extremely rugged. These served as bulwarks for Grant.

The attack was begun at daylight, on Sherman and Prentiss's divisions. They, however, were quite ready, the skirmishes of the last few days having warned them of the possibility of such an event. Prentiss formed his division *outside of his camps, and there received the assault.* Sherman too was prepared, and the whole command was rapidly under arms. It was necessary indeed to do their utmost, for the onslaught was fierce. There were not more than thirty-three thousand national troops on the ground, Lewis Wallace being five miles off. Grant was breakfasting at Savanna, when he heard the earliest firing; his horse was already saddled for him to go out in search of Buell, but the artillery at once proclaimed a heavy engagement. He instantly sent word to Nelson to hurry up his command to the river, opposite Pittsburg, and started himself by steamer for the Landing. On the way he stopped at Crump's Landing, and in person directed Lewis Wallace to hold himself in readiness for orders to march to Pittsburg. Grant arrived on the field at eight o'clock, and found affairs looking black indeed. Neither Sherman nor Prentiss had been able to hold his own. Their troops were raw, and both divisions had been obliged to fall back. McClernand, however, was moved promptly to the support of Sherman, and Hurlbut reinforced Prentiss. W. H. L. Wallace was also moved to support the centre of the line, and the fight now became confused and terrific in the extreme. The country was broken, half covered with forest, and the evolutions of troops difficult. Sherman's left finally broke entirely, despite the desperate exertions of its commander, and a panic ensued that spread to thousands in the national ranks. Repeated orders were sent to hurry up the divisions of Nelson and Lewis Wallace, but those commands did not appear. Prentiss's division became exposed, its commander neglecting to withdraw, although the troops on each side of him were compelled to fall back; and late in the afternoon he was surrounded and taken prisoner with four regiments. This calamity disheartened many, and a crowd of fugitives, amounting to six or seven thousand, fled from the field to the gunboats. Those who remained, however, did their duty nobly. Grant was on every part of the field, exposing himself to the thickest of the fire, and encouraging both men and officers. He was struck on the ankle once, but not hurt. Sherman and the other division commanders all displayed energy and courage. Grant felt the greatest anxiety for the arrival of Lewis Wallace and Nelson, and sent messenger after messenger to bring up those commanders, but neither of them arrived. Nelson had a bad road to move over, but, although ordered to start at seven o'clock in the morning, for some unexplained cause, he failed to do so until one in the afternoon. After that he made all expedition. Lewis Wallace took the wrong road, and marched in a direction that led him away from the field.

About two o'clock General Buell came on the field in person. He had heard the cannonading, and at once set about urging on his troops, two more divisions of which had arrived at Savanna. He reached Pittsburg at a moment when Grant happened to be at the Landing, endeavoring to stay the tide of runaways coming in from the front. It seemed to Buell that all was lost, and he asked Grant, "What preparations have you made for retreating, general?" This idea, however, had not presented itself to that officer, and he quietly replied, "*I hav'nt despaired of whipping them yet.*" "No, of course," said Buell. "But, if you should be whipped, how will you get your men across the river? These transports will not take more than ten thousand troops." "*If I have to retreat,*" replied Grant, "*ten thou-sand will be as many as I shall need transports for.*"

Grant indeed always made his defence an offensive one. He was one of those soldiers who *never* despair of whipping the enemy, even when things look most gloomy. This confidence and obstinacy combined it was that made him ready to take advantage of every chance, and out of the very jaws of defeat to wrest victory. He believed that in every battle the combatants reach a point when each side is almost overcome, and the leader who then makes an almost superhuman effort is sure to turn the scales in his own favor. That effort he was always ready to make, just when other men give up in despair. In the blackest crisis his faculties seemed most brilliant, at the most exhausting moment his strength was renewed with greatest vigor. When all depended upon holding out a little longer, or upon some wonderful inspiration that should suggest the salvation of an army, he was sure to hold out, the inspiration never failed. He who ordinarily was almost phlegmatic, unimpassioned, what some call dull, then was sharp, clear, decided, commanding not only men but events, bending even the enemy to his plans, seeing what they must be doing, and knowing what should be done to thwart them, and doing it. It was so at Donelson, where he turned the tide of disaster into success, divining in an instant the intention of the rebels from the apparently trivial circumstance of the haversacks, and perceiving (not a minute too late, as so many others do,) that the way to stem the advance on his right was to attack furiously at the other end of the line. The result was Smith's charge, and the capture of the fort.

So at Shiloh, where he was outnumbered; where thousands of his men failed him; where his army was driven back by hard fighting, driven back for hours and for miles; where Buell was thinking of retreat, and many generals would have prepared for surrender. But, if his troops were driven back, Grant's spirits were not; if some were beaten, he was thinking of "*whipping 'em yet,*" and at four o'clock on this dreadful day, he gave orders to Sherman for an attack on the morrow. There was a lull just then, as there had been at Donelson. The rebels had nearly won, but jaded, exhausted, they stopped to breathe, and Grant, *before he knew of the arrival of Buell's column*, was preparing to take the initiative in the morning. For such a man, defeat was impossible. This peculiarity extorted the warmest admiration from his great friend, Sherman, who said, "This faith gave you victory at Shiloh;" "The simple faith in success you have always manifested, which I can liken to nothing else than the faith a Christian has in the Saviour." "I tell you it was this that made us act with confidence; I knew, wherever I was, that you thought of me, and if I got in a tight place you would help me out, if alive." "Until you had won Donelson, I was almost cowed, but that admitted a ray of light I have followed since."

But the rebel commander was killed, and his successor, Beauregard, lacked just this quality which distinguished Grant. He made one last attempt to drive the national troops into the river, and failing in this, drew off, to wait till morning. Two of Nelson's regiments, the head of his column, came up at this juncture, but their arrival was unknown to Beauregard; darkness came on just as they crossed the Tennessee, and both armies slept on the field. All night long, Buell's army continued to arrive; all night Grant was posting them. He gave the fresh troops the extreme left, nearest the river and the bulk of the enemy, and reformed the shattered battalions that had fought so hard on Sunday. He visited each division commander himself, the rain falling in torrents. The troops were drenched. The gunboats kept up an incessant fire on the enemy, and the mingled storm of rain and shell was as terrible as the heat of the battle of yesterday. Lewis Wallace arrived soon after nightfall, and was given the extreme right.

At daybreak Grant attacked with vigor all along his new line. Twenty thousand reinforcements had reached him, and the presence of this immense addition was felt at once. It was soon evident that the tables were turned. The rebels, so exultant the day before, were now hard pressed themselves. All the ground, all the camps and guns they had won, were regained. Still the fighting was desperate. It was a great conflict between Southern impetuosity and Northern determination. It was this on both days, but on the former day that determination, incarnated as it was in Grant, stood up against the odds; and on the second, the rebel impetuosity succumbed when outnumbered. About two o'clock Beauregard withdrew from the field.

One of the last encounters occurred as the First Ohio volunteers were moving across a field near Grant. Another regiment near by was hard pressed, and Grant stopped the First Ohio, and himself ordered it to charge in support of the endangered force. He rode with it in the line of battle, the men cheering him with enthusiasm. Both regiments were fired at the sight; they pressed on, Grant with them, drove the rebels in their front, and seized one of the last positions yet maintained by the enemy.

The rain had again begun to fall heavily, darkness was now approaching, the troops were frightfully exhausted with the extraordinary efforts of the two days, but a force was sent out in pursuit of Beauregard. He, however, had got so far that it was not judged expedient to follow in force. Grant lost in the two days' battle one thousand seven hundred killed, and over ten thousand wounded and missing. Beauregard reported one thousand seven hundred and twenty-eight killed, and nine thousand wounded and missing. And thus the great effort of the rebels to assume the offensive at the West was defeated; the most furious onslaught they ever made was repelled. The loyal West was saved from invasion. The mightiest armament the enemy had got together in that part of the theatre of war was driven back. Beauregard telegraphed his government, "we retired to our entrenchments *at Corinth, which we can hold.*" On the 8th, he asked permission from Grant to bury his dead on the field, but the Union commander had already performed the task.

Notwithstanding the fact that Grant's unshakable steadiness and determination had proved the salvation of his army and of the entire West, there were not wanting those who maligned him bitterly on account of the battle of Shiloh. At various times in his career, he, like most other men of genius and virtue, has been the target of bitter and violent abuse. The best patriots of the American Revolution were not exempt, Washington himself suffering as much from the tongues and pens of recreant countrymen as the blackest character of the day; and it was not to be supposed that Grant, now rising rapidly to eminence and fame, could escape the penalty which greatness always has to pay. Envy, ingratitude, hatred, calumny, did their worst. After the brilliant success at Donelson, symptoms of this at once appeared. Men above and below him in military rank sought even then to supplant him in the estimation of the public, attributed his triumph to others or to fortune, and charged him with faults and vices which they hoped would obscure the lustre of his

deeds. The result has been shown; he was relieved from his command, immediately after the most splendid victory that had then been
won by our arms. But this could not last, and he was forced back
by public opinion into the place that he had earned. After Shiloh,
however, came a still more violent outbreak. He was assailed on all
sides for his conduct in a battle where his greatest qualities were as
conspicuous as they have ever been before or since; where his own
personal exertions saved the nation from crushing defeat; where he
held up the drooping spirits and sustained the flagging energies of
both officers and men, under circumstances that appalled many of
the bravest hearts; where disaster seemed so inevitable that a distinguished soldier, just arriving on the field, and who had not gone
through the terrible conflict of the day, yet getting a glimpse of the
battle, inquired, at once, "What dispositions have you made for
retreat?" so unavoidable did further disaster seem; when even Sherman was surprised at being ordered to renew the fight, while thousands
of his soldiers were flying in panic, and reinforcements were yet far
off. Yet for this unconquerable spirit which enabled him to hold
those who retained heart steadily to their work, and finally gave him
victory, the hero at first received no credit. His immediate superior
sought to attribute what had been done to Sherman, wresting Grant's
own magnanimous acknowledgments of Sherman's undoubted services, into a means to injure the man who had so used those services
as to achieve success where success seemed almost unattainable; as
if, on a field where five division commanders were engaged, and Sherman never left the extreme right, he could possibly have accomplished
the whole result, which it required all the management of the five
divisions and the personal presence of a commander over all, to
achieve. Sherman himself never claimed what Halleck sought to
thrust upon him. As generously as Smith at Donelson, who said
"No congratulations are due me, I simply obeyed orders," Sherman
took pains to ascribe to his commander, the results which he knew had
been so hardly earned. Yet, after Donelson, Halleck urged the Government to promote Smith, the inferior, over Grant to a major gener-
alcy. "Honor *him* for this victory." "Make *him* a major general.
You can't get a better one." "Smith turned the tide." And after
Shiloh, he boldly declared to the Government that Sherman had
"secured the fortunes of the day."
    He did more than this. He came direct to the field from Missouri,
and assumed command of the two armies, deposing Grant even from

his old command. He gave him, indeed, an ostensible position, but contrived to make it evident to himself and all under him, that he was in disgrace. Grant being second in rank after Halleck, was necessarily made second in command, but this was merely nominal; orders were not sent through him, he was not informed of movements, he was not invited to councils of war; when he did offer advice or opinion it was spurned, and his own subordinates in his very presence, held whispered consultations from which he was excluded. This course naturally reacted upon the country, and the land rang with tirades against its greatest general on account of one of his greatest deeds. He was accused of error in posting his troops on the west bank of the river, when, in the first place, the troops were posted there before he took command, and by that accomplished soldier C. F. Smith; and in the second place, Grant's judgment in retaining them there has been approved, not only by Smith and Sherman, and his own maturer experience, but by that of all good military critics since. He was accused of negligence in allowing himself to be surprised, when, in fact, he had exercised unusual vigilance; getting all his divisions in readiness, so that commanders had their horses saddled in case of an attack, on the very morning when the battle occurred, and his pickets were doubled and his grand guards pushed out a mile and a half, the night before; when the rebel leader himself declared that he encountered Grant in force at the encampments of his advanced position; and official reports show that the division commander who was first attacked received the assault outside of his camps.

Grant naturally was mortified and indignant at the injustice which he suffered, both from the country and his superiors. The former he endured in silence, sure that in the end he would be righted; but the constant humiliations to which he was subjected in camp, came home to the soldier's heart. His little headquarters followed the course of the army in its onward movement to Corinth, but it might as well have been in Ohio. He repeatedly asked to be relieved from duty, but his request was not granted, and after one indignity, more pointed than usual, he was even on the brink of resigning. Sherman, however, his tried and trusted friend, who knew how little all of this was deserved, and was confident that the great man would yet show to the world all the great qualities which he recognized, comforted him and dissuaded him. It was but a momentary impulse, and Grant determined to endure still longer "the insolence of office, and the spurns that patient merit of the unworthy takes."

CORINTH.

For nearly two months after Shiloh, the army was occupied in moving eighteen miles. Halleck's imagination was so inflamed by what he heard of the battle of Shiloh, that he only advanced behind breastworks, although all his officers and men were restless under the unwonted restraint. The enemy made no show of opposition, but the cautious commander could not be persuaded to attack, although he had been reinforced till his army was over a hundred thousand strong, and at least double that of the rebels. But at last he arrived in front of Corinth, and now the soldiers were impatient for assault. Still Halleck was afraid of being attacked. Grant went to him one day, and suggested an offensive movement, but with no avail; and finally, on the 30th of May, Corinth fell into Halleck's hands, having been evacuated by the rebels several days before. While Halleck had been lying idle in front of the works, the rebels amused him with a show of strength, and decamped with their entire army, stores, and ordnance. A pursuit was ordered, from which Grant was excluded, but it was ineffectual, and terminated in a few days.

In July, Halleck was ordered to Washington, to take command of all the armies. Grant was next in rank in all the West, and entitled to command the army which Halleck left; but the old hostility still continued, and the latter offered the command to Colonel Allen, a quartermaster, proposing to get the requisite rank for him if he would accept the offer. Allen, however, declined the promotion, and then only, Halleck allowed Grant to take the command which was his by virtue of seniority, as well as services. This fact was not disclosed to Grant. The army, however, was greatly broken up. Buell was sent further east, and Grant was left with not more than thirty or forty thousand men to guard all the region from the Mississippi to the Tennessee, and from the Ohio as far south as Corinth. As soon as the rebels discovered that his force was thus depleted, they made every effort to annoy him, and his attention was devoted to defending himself in half a dozen different places at once, with an inferior force.

IUKA.

Twenty one miles east of Corinth, is a town called Iuka, which was held by national troops, but on the 13th of September this was seized

3

by a force of rebels under Price, and Grant at once determined to dislodge and capture them. He collected his troops from various parts of his command, ordering General Rosecranz to march east, on the south side of the railroad which connects Corinth and Iuka, and Ord on the north side. These forces were to attack Iuka simultaneously, from the different directions indicated, and Rosecranz was especially ordered to secure the only two roads leading south, so that no avenue of escape should be left to the rebels. Price had about ten or twelve thousand men, Ord had eight thousand, and Rosecranz nine thousand. Grant would therefore be able, by concentrating, to outnumber the enemy, who, however, was superior, to either of the national detachments. The roads were difficult and widely separated, and Grant remained a few miles in the rear of both divisions, so as to be able to communicate directly with each and to control them simultaneously. On the 18th of September, Ord was within four miles of Iuka on the north, but Rosecranz did not succeed this day in getting within twenty miles of the town, thus greatly disappointing Grant. Ord was therefore instructed not to attack him, until he heard the firing of Rosecranz's guns on the south.

It was late in the afternoon of the 19th when Rosecranz reached Iuka, and his movements then were betrayed to the enemy by a spy. He did not succeed in occupying more than one of the roads leading south. The rebels learning of this, and fearing the concentration which Grant had planned, withdrew from Ord's front, massed on the single road by which Rosecranz was advancing, and checked the head of his column. He fought vigorously, but was unable to make any advance, and the battle lasted till dark. While Price was thus holding Rosecranz on one road, he sent off everything from the town by the other, which Rosecranz had failed to occupy, and in the night the entire rebel army withdrew. The next morning Ord and Rosecranz marched into the town, but the enemy had escaped. Ord had not heard any noise of the firing the day before, as the wind blew heavily towards the south, and Rosecranz could not inform Grant of the battle until it was over.

SECOND SIEGE OF CORINTH.

But although Grant's plan was not carried out, he yet had prevented the enemy from advancing eastward, which was very important at that juncture. The rebels now continued the strategy which had already occasioned him so much uneasiness. He still had not force enough to assume the offensive, and was compelled to content himself with discovering the plans of the rebels and merely checking their movements. This was the more disagreeable to him, as he was unaccustomed to defensive operations. His nature always impelled him to attack, and now that such a course was impossible, he was distressed and annoyed. Still, he did the best practicable with the means and opportunities at his control. He could not concentrate his troops at any one point, lest he should leave some other place exposed to a prompt and wary enemy; he was obliged, therefore, to hold himself in readiness overywhere, so as to move to the quarter first threatened or attacked. He was thus kept on the alert for several weeks, but finally became convinced that Corinth had been selected by the rebels for assault.

His own headquarters were at this time at Jackson, Tennessee, a place central to his entire command. He had previously directed that the defences of Corinth should be carefully strengthened; indeed, almost entirely reconstructed, and placed Rosecranz in command there with about nineteen thousand men. He now ordered Generals Ord and Hurlbut, with several thousand troops, to move so as to strike the rebel column on its way to Corinth. The enemy it was probable would move eastward on Corinth, and Ord was to come from the north so as to attack in flank or rear. All happened exactly as Grant had planned. The rebels attacked in great force on the 3d of October, appearing on the western side of Corinth. They drove Rosecranz's forces inside the works on this day, and on the 4th attempted to carry the town. At first they met with some success, but when they came near the new works which had been constructed by Grant some weeks before, their advance was checked, and finally converted into a rout.

Now became apparent the wisdom of Grant's strategy. The fleeing enemy suddenly came upon Ord's command, waiting for just this emergency, and another fight ensued, in which severe damage was again inflicted on the rebels. They received severe injury on each day, but Ord's command was much too small to do more than check them, even defeated as they were, so they turned to another road, and escaped with the fragments that had been saved.

The strategy of these two little battles displayed nearly the same principles which Grant afterwards developed so brilliantly on a larger stage. This was the first time when he had occasion to make combinations of troops on different fields. Heretofore, all that had been necessary was to bring up his men, and handle them skilfully when they arrived in the presence of the enemy. At Donelson, it was indeed the very genius of tactics which inspired the attack on the left, at the critical moment, in order to relieve the hard-pressed battalions of the right. At Belmont, it was great determination and real soldiership, to "*Cut our way out as we cut our way in.*" As Sherman long afterwards wrote to Grant: "At Belmont, you manifested your traits; at Donelson, also, you illustrated your whole character;" and at Shiloh it had been pure grit that held the enemy at bay, that would not be conquered, and that finally took up the fight again and carried it on to victory. But at Corinth and Iuka Grant's share was strategical; he planned all the movements until the troops came in the presence of the enemy; he directed the concentration, and pointed out the lines upon which it should take place. It was generalship, not mere soldiering, that he evinced here. His intellectual, rather than his moral qualities were called into play; and the attentive student, either of the character of the man, or simply of military operations, will discover in this campaign the same ability, of course on a smaller scale, that enabled him to conceive the brilliant operations at Vicksburg, to concert and execute the complicated movements which resulted so splendidly at Chattanooga, and afterwards to control all the armies of the Republic with a single aim, and make the movements of hundreds of thousands of men, separated sometimes by thousands of miles, all tend to the accomplishment of one design. The unity of purpose, the concentration of scattered forces, the bringing to bear on a greater body of the enemy two or three smaller forces, which in the aggregate were larger than the entire rebel strength—this is the very essence of generalship; this implies ability of the highest and rarest class.

These movements relieved Grant from any further necessity for acting on the defensive. The double check administered to the enemy, although not so complete as he had designed or desired, yet drove the rebels back, and gave him a chance to take the initiative, a part to which his judgment and his nature always inclined. He always preferred to make his enemies fight on ground that he had selected, and at times when he was prepared: his career always illustrated the ancient saying: "If you are a great general, come out of your works and fight me." "If *you* are a great general, *make me* come out of my works and fight you." His plans after this always included the operations of the enemy; the campaigns were fought *as* he wished and *when* he wished, and luckily for America, they *resulted as he wished.* Sometimes the result was long delayed, but it never failed in the end to realize his most sanguine expectations. But this all the world knows. He got, however, little credit for his strategy in this campaign. The high officers of the army could not understand how so quiet a man could be a great one. He had not graduated near the head of his class; how, then, could he understand military science? He made no parade of his knowledge of books; he never compared himself with Napoleon; he never discussed Cæsar or Wellington. How, then, could he know what it was indispensable to know? The idea of his possessing intuitive genius had not occurred to them. *They* had to learn rules and principles out of books, and could not always apply them afterwards; how was it to be supposed that this unassuming, modest soldier could get, out of his own brain, combinations and ideas superior to what accomplished men had derived from long study of famous fields and renowned generals. But Grant, instead of being one of those who act according to rules and precedents, belonged to the class that invents rules and establishes precedents. He was not a student, because he was original. Other people will have hereafter to study his campaigns, but he acted, of his own instinct, on the self-same principles that other great conquerors discovered and applied in other theatres. He never stopped to consider what Napoleon or Frederick would have done, under similar circumstances, nor tried to recollect the strategy of Ulm or the tactics of Jena. He made a new strategy and a new tactics for himself, just as Frederick or Wellington would have done, had they been at Donelson or Shiloh, based all the while on the same immutable principles which are at the bottom of all science. He hardly knew that he did this himself; he was unconscious of his own powers. Like the countryman in the play, who had been speaking prose without knowing it, he achieved greatness unawares. He did the best he knew how, and it was the best that could be done. He applied the highest principles of military science, just as Shakespeare wrote Hamlet and Othello, without referring to books or models. This is genius.

Not that he was ignorant. The fact of his graduating at West Point is proof of his acquaintance with the technicalities of his art. But he was not given to relying on the past. He knew enough of the past and of the doing of other great commanders to appreciate the fact that they had carved out greatness by being self-reliant, by originating new ideas under new circumstances, by casting behind them the trammels of the schools; and the influence he received from them was sufficient to make him like them in this respect. He followed their examples by rejecting precedents and ignoring rules whenever he thought them inapplicable. He was infused with the same spirit that penetrated them, and by refusing to copy, he came to rival them.

OXFORD.

Immediately after the repulse of the rebel assault on Corinth, Grant proposed to the Government that he should be allowed to move on Vicksburg. The national forces had driven the rebels from every important position on the Mississippi north of Vicksburg, but there the enemy had concentrated his strength and determined to make a stand. Grant's idea now was to move down through the State of Mississippi, in rear of the town, and force its evacuation. Hitherto the attempt had been to attack it in front. Not receiving any reply to his suggestion, Grant prepared to make his campaign without orders; but as soon as Halleck learned that his subordinate had really started, he sent him the sanction desired.

Grant moved on the 2d of November, with thirty thousand men, from Grand Junction, a place on the railroad which connects Corinth and Memphis, and about half way between the eastern and western boundaries of Mississippi. He meant to march south, along the line of the Mississippi Central railroad ; but the rebels destroyed the road in his front as he advanced, and he was obliged to repair it while moving, for he had no other means of supplying his troops. At this time it was not supposed possible for an army to advance more than two or three days beyond its base. This impossibility Grant afterwards found a means of obviating, but he learned the means from experience ; and, at the time we speak of, he had not discovered all the advantages of a movable column, nor the practicability of subsisting without supplies carried with him, or else drawn direct from his own base. It was this campaign which taught him the lesson, or rather which created the necessity that he proceeded to supply. At first he moved slowly, because of the delay occasioned by rebuilding bridges and repairing roads. The enemy was immediately in his front, but made no serious opposition. Grant was also retarded by contradictory reports about his own command, and in fact by confused orders from Washington.

Major General McClernand, an officer who had been promoted

direct from civil life, utterly without military talent or acquirement, was striving to obtain the command now intrusted to Grant. He had political influence and great ambition, and finally succeeded in procuring a part of Grant's troops. The latter heard of these machinations, and was embarrassed in his advance by the probability of any day hearing that he had been superseded, or at least that a part of his command was to be taken from him at a critical moment. Halleck was on Grant's side in this matter, and strove to prevent the injudicious interference. For a while he succeeded, and, when Grant arrived at Holly Springs, twenty-five miles from Grand Junction, the general-in-chief dispatched, "You have command of all troops sent to your department, and permission to fight the enemy when you please."

Grant accordingly ordered Sherman, who was at Memphis, to move out from that place with ten or twelve thousand men, and join him at Oxford, beyond the Tallahatchie, and twenty-five miles or more south of Holly Springs. A coöperative movement was at the same time directed by Halleck, by which a force from Arkansas was to be sent in rear of the rebels to distract their attention from Grant. By the 5th of December, Grant was at Oxford, the rebels having evacuated their works on the Tallahatchie river, and the entire Mississippi Central road up to that place having fallen into his hands, along with one thousand two hundred prisoners.

The same day Halleck ordered him not to attempt to hold the country south of the Tallahatchie, but to collect twenty-five thousand troops at Memphis, with a view to sending them down the Mississippi to attack Vicksburg in front. Grant immediately determined to send Sherman to command this expedition, having received the permission to move his troops as he thought best. He accordingly dispatched Sherman back to Memphis, from which place he was to move his command on transports to the mouth of the Yazoo river, which empties into the Mississippi nine miles above Vicksburg. Sherman was to be joined at this place by Admiral Porter with a fleet of gunboats, and the two together were to provide a new base for Grant, who would march on so as to strike the Yazoo farther up its course; or, if this plan could not be carried out, Grant was to hold the enemy in his front in the interior, while Sherman would attack Vicksburg.

Preparations for this combined movement were proceeding rapidly, when Grant finally received orders to give McClernand the command of the river expedition. This was a terrible blow to him, for neither

ho, Porter, Sherman, Halleck, nor any of the prominent officers at
the West, had any confidence in McClernand's ability. There was,
however, nothing left but to obey, and Grant the same day wrote to
McClernand to assume command; but, before his orders could reach
the latter, the enemy interfered. A large force from the rebel column
in Grant's front was sent to his rear, to cut his communications at several points, and to destroy his secondary base of supplies at Holly
Springs. Grant had been informed in advance, of this intention of
the rebels, and had promptly notified his subordinates in the rear, of
their danger, instructing them to hold out at all hazards. All obeyed
but one, and the enemy was repulsed at every point except at Holly
Springs, the most important of all. The officer in command there
was false to his trust, and surrendered without a fight, and the rebels
entirely destroyed the vast accumulation of stores which Grant had
collected there, as well as the railroads and bridges in the vicinity.
They were unable, however, to remain in the place. Still, the tempo-
rary capture was a great disaster; the impossibility of holding so long
and exposed a line in an enemy's country was demonstrated, and
Grant at once saw the necessity of falling back. The rebels in his
front made no offensive demonstration, but he asked permission immediately to assume command of the river expedition. As it was not to
be intrusted to Sherman, he was anxious himself to direct it.

But, although he moved back to Holly Springs as rapidly as possible, it was necessary to live until the new supplies could be brought
forward, and Grant at once determined to take stores from the country. This the rebels had not anticapated, and the announcement
struck them with terror. The disloyal inhabitants had been jubilant
over the interruption of Grant's communications and the destruction
of his supplies; but, when the deficiency had to be made good from
their own barns, their delight was turned to dismay. They petitioned
against this course, but in vain; Grant was compelled to subsist his
troops, and had no other resources than those he found in the country. These were abundant, and the army lived well.

This was the lesson he learned, far more important than any results
attained by the enemy. It was this which he afterwards applied
behind Vicksburg; it was this which changed the entire character of
the war, and initiated one of the most marked peculiarities of Grant's
mode of campaigning. From this experience he gained the idea
which was afterwards developed into some of the greatest achievements in military history; which afforded suggestions not only to

Grant himself, but, after he had applied them, to two of his greatest subordinates, Sherman and Sheridan, and contributed to the success of their most brilliant campaigns.

Meanwhile Sherman had started from Memphis before McClernand arrived to supersede him. The delay in transmitting Grant's orders, which had been occasioned by the break in communication, gave Sherman time to perfect his arrangements. He left Memphis with thirty-thousand men, and at Helena was reinforced by twelve thousand more. On the 27th of December he debarked his troops on the south bank of the Yazoo, near its mouth, and under convoy of Admiral Porter's fleet of gunboats. A steep line of hills runs along the left bank of the Yazoo at this place, covering Vicksburg, which itself lies on the face of a declivitous bluff rising abruptly from the Mississippi. These hills were all defended by batteries, and in front of the Yazoo face, the country was cut up with swamps and creeks, so as to be almost impassable. Sherman nevertheless succeeded in getting his men across this difficult ground, and assaulted the hills with great vigor. The natural and artificial strength of the works, however, was so great, that the attack failed, and the men withdrew to the transports, after a loss of one thousand eight hundred men in killed, wounded, and missing.

The combined effort against Vicksburg was thus unsuccessful at both extremities. Grant was unable to continue his southward march in the interior, and Sherman was repelled from the works on the Yazoo. When the latter moved out of the Yazoo into the Mississippi, he was met by McClernand, who at once assumed supreme command.

WEST OF VICKSBURG.

Grant, however, arrived at Memphis by the 10th of January, and was now authorized by the Government either to take command of the expedition himself, or to appoint whomever he chose instead. He was determined now to throw all his forces on the river, as it was evident that he could not maintain his communications if he attempted again to advance in the centre of the State. A much smaller force could at any time cut his line and destroy stores that it had taken him months to accumulate. On the 17th of January, he visited his forces at the mouth of the Yazoo, and at once decided that the troops must get below the city to be used effectually. He therefore set about collecting all the men he could spare from Kentucky and Tennessee, and from northern Mississippi, abandoning many positions in the interior, of less importance, and began in earnest the mighty task of opening the Mississippi river. At first he thought of putting Sherman in command of the expedition, but in consideration of the fact that Sherman was junior to McClernand, he finally judged it best to obviate all criticism, and, by virtue of his own rank, and the authority of the President, to assume himself immediate command. This he did on the 29th of January, 1863.

The failure of one plan never discouraged Grant. He had not been successful in the first movements against Vicksburg, but that was simply an incentive to him to make another effort. The same spirit which he had manifested at Belmont when he was surrounded, at Donelson when his right was repulsed, at Shiloh when his whole army was driven back two miles, animated him still. The very day that his communications were cut at Holly Springs, through the cowardice or treachery of a subordinate, he began his preparations for the campaign on the Mississippi. Vicksburg was the great stronghold of rebellion at the West. It barred and commanded the great river; when it fell, the Mississippi would be opened. As long as it stood, the strength of the insurgents was defiant; the Northwest was cut off from the sea. Here, it was apparent, the struggle must be fought for the mastery of the West. The rebels spent their best energies in fortifying and strengthening what they called the Gibraltar of America. They threw immense bodies of troops into the State of Mississippi, to defend and to cover the town; they sent their best generals to command these troops; they boldly proclaimed Vicksburg to be impregnable.

The town stands on the eastern bank of the Mississippi, about nine miles south of the mouth of the Yazoo. Both rivers are circuitous in a remarkable degree. The Mississippi turns and winds so that it runs towards every point of the compass within a distance of twenty miles. Just below the mouth of the Yazoo one of the most extraordinary of these bends occurs, the river running first southeast, then northeast, and then with a sudden curve turning to the southwest. Vicksburg is situated just south of this last bend, on a long line of bluffs that stretches from the Yazoo southwest for fifty miles. These hills rise several hundred feet above the level of the stream, and reach two or three miles into the interior. They are extremely rugged and precipitous, particularly towards the river, so that the streets in Vicksburg are built in terraces one above the other, to the summit of the ridge.

The entire country on both banks of the Mississippi, outside of this narrow line of hills, is one great marsh, thickly overgrown with underbrush and forest trees, and intersected with innumerable shallow streams, a region about as unfit for offensive military operations as it is possible to conceive. This country was now completely flooded by the great rise in the Mississippi, and the water stood to the depth of several feet, everywhere except on the bluffs, and along the narrow artificial banks called levees, erected by the inhabitants to protect their lands from the annual inundation. This year the deluge was greater than had been known for many seasons.

' The works reached south from the Yazoo to a point on the Mississippi called Warrenton, a distance of twenty miles. They were defended on the water side by twenty-eight guns, which commanded all approach by the river. Every effort had been made to strengthen the fortifications. Nature herself had done her best to render Vicksburg impregnable; these abrupt hills overlooking a flat country for miles, the country submerged in water, a great river immediately in front of the ridge, were in themselves extraordinary obstacles; but when to these were added an army of sixty thousand men, either in the town or in the region covering it, and all available for its defence; rifle-pits, formidable forts, obstructions in the river, and an armament of over two hundred cannon, the difficulties in the way of Grant seemed almost insurmountable. To oppose them he had a force at this time of about fifty thousand troops—the Fifteenth corps under Sherman, the Thirteenth under McClernand, and the Seventeenth under McPherson. Admiral Porter's coöperating fleet of gunboats numbered sixty vessels of all classes, carrying two hundred and eighty guns. Not half of these, however, were retained near Vicksburg; the others were occupied in patrolling the river to Cairo, a distance of over six hundred miles. For Grant drew all his supplies of men, ordnance, and rations from St. Louis and Cairo, and the river was infested with guerrillas, who fired from the banks on every passing steamer, whenever the gunboat protection was withdrawn.

Grant's first business was to get a footing on the eastern bank of the river, where his troops could be established on dry land; but the rebels held every foot of tenable ground, and it was impossible to attack them in front with any chance of success. The gunboats could be of no assistance, for the enemy had a plunging fire, and could rake the river in every direction, and transports could not approach close enough to land troops, as a single shot might sink a steamer with her

whole freight of soldiers. A landing had already been tried by Sherman on the Yazoo, twelve miles above the town, where the line of
bluffs strikes that river at Haines' Bluff; but though conducted with
skill and gallantry, it had signally failed in January, so that it seemed
as if Grant's ordinary strategy of direct and bold attack must now be
abandoned.

The resources of his genius, however, were not limited to the expe-
dients which he preferred. If he could not do what he desired, he
was always willing to do what he was able. The nature of the country
now suggested various schemes. First of all it was determined to dig
a canal across the peninsula formed by the bend in the river in front
of ·Vicksburg. The land on the opposite side runs out in the shape
of a tongue not more than a mile or two across; the plan was to cut
through this, and let the waters of the Mississippi in, so far from the
town that transports could pass through this artificial channel into the
river below Vicksburg, and land troops on the south side of the city.
The engineers hoped that the whole course of the river might be
diverted from its usual direction by this canal, or at least that sufficient water could be induced to run through, to float vessels of draught
sufficient for Grant's purposes.

Accordingly, for two months thousands of soldiers and negroes were
at work digging, in full sight of the besieged city. The troops were
encamped all along the west bank of the river immediately behind the
levees. Their tents were frequently submerged by the water, which
yet showed no appearance or promise of subsidence, and disease made
sad havoc among the soldiers. The tedious work, however, was prosecuted till the 8th of March, the canal was almost complete, when an
additional and rapid rise in the river broke the dam near the upper
end of the canal, and an irresistible torrent poured over the whole
peninsula, broke the levee, submerged all the camps, and spread for
miles into the interior. The troops had to flee for their lives. Futile
attempts were immediately made to repair the damage, but on the 27th
of March the plan was finally abandoned, it being ascertained that the
rebels had erected new batteries, which would completely command
the southern exit from the canal, and had even already driven out the
dredge-boats working there.

While this stupendous endeavor to convert one of the natural features of the continent into an engine of war was being prosecuted,
Grant was directing still another attempt, if possible more Titanic
than the other. Seventy miles above Vicksburg, on the west side of

the Mississippi, is an inland lake, formed by the old bed of the river, and a mile distant from the present channel. This is named Lake Providence, and is connected with various streams, or bayous as they are called in this region, which in their turn interlace and intersect, forming an interrupted communication at last with the Tensas, and from the Tensas with the Washita, and finally the Red river, which itself empties into the Mississippi four hundred miles below Vicksburg. The plan was to cut a canal a mile long, from the Mississippi into Lake Providence, so as to let in the waters of the great river; then to improve the navigation of these various tortuous and shallow creeks in the interior of Louisiana, to clear away trees, dig out swamps, deepen channels, until an absolute water-course should be opened into the Red river, so that the army might be moved on transports through these bayous into the Mississippi below, and then be able to march up and reach Vicksburg, on the southern side. It was, however, found impossible to procure a sufficient number of light-draught steamers to carry an army through these shallow streams; and this plan, which rivalled the famous boast of Xerxes, that he would march his armies over the sea and sail them over the land, was abandoned, about the same time with its counterpart, the canal.

NORTH OF VICKSBURG.

It was the impossibility of marching troops over the submerged swamps that made Grant's principal difficulty. If it had not been for this, he could at once have moved along the western bank; but neither men nor artillery nor stores could be got through the inundated region; so that still another of these extraordinary amphibious undertakings was begun; this one on the eastern side. The Yazoo pass is a narrow creek, three hundred miles above Vicksburg, which formerly connected Moon lake with the Mississippi river. The lake is similar to Lake Providence, having been formed by the windings of the Mississippi, which every now and then deviates from its ancient course, and leaves a bed of standing water, miles away from its more recent channel. Moon lake is connected with two or three large and navigable streams; the Cold Water, the Tallahatchie, and the Yallabusha, which finally unite and form the Yazoo. The plan was to cut the levee which interrupted the flow of the Mississippi into Yazoo pass, and then, through these devious windings, to carry troops into the Yazoo, to the hills above Vicksburg, and so get the army on dry land.

The scheme was prosecuted with great vigor; the streams were deeper and wider than on the western side, and the plan promised more success. But the rebels soon discovered the attempt, and hewed large trees into the rivers to obstruct the advance. Troops on transports, under cover of gunboats, were sent into the pass, and, after infinite trouble and delay, succeeded in removing these obstructions. But while this was going on, the enemy set to work fortifying, and at the junction of the two rivers which form the Yazoo, hundreds of miles from the Mississippi, they erected a formidable work called Fort Pemberton. Here the elements again defended treason, for the waters were so high, and the country all around so low, that no troops could be landed to attack the fort. The gunboats made three attempts to silence its guns, but the tortuous character of the stream was such that they could not approach it properly for their purposes, and this attempt also failed. Nothing was able to pass Fort Pemberton. Grant had by this time sent several thousand men into the pass, and was making preparations to move an entire corps in the same direction, when the utter impracticability of this route was demonstrated.

The rebels, however, found this out as early as he, and sent troops in large numbers to destroy or cut off the Union force already in the pass; and in order to distract them from this purpose, Grant inaugurated still another movement. Nearer to Vicksburg than the Yazoo pass, and on the same side of the river, is another intricate network of bayous, connecting the Mississippi with the Yazoo. These creeks are more tortuous and difficult, by far, than those which constitute the pass; they are choked up with trees; so narrow that the branches from each side are interlaced, and so crooked that it seemed impossible to navigate them. But Grant conferred with Admiral Porter, and, after making a reconnoissance himself, determined to send Sherman up this route, so as, if possible, to strike the Yazoo river below the point where the rebel fort had been built, and thus not only extricate the Union troops who had gone in from above, but threaten the rebel forces in the interior, who would thus be placed between two national detachments.

The difficulties encountered on this route, which was called the Steele's bayou route, from one of the creeks on the way, far transcended any of those which obstructed the other expeditions. But Sherman and Porter pushed on; the gunboats went in advance, to force, by their heavier weight, a passage through the trees, so that the steamers carrying troops might follow. For miles there was no hard land where soldiers could march; and the creeks were so narrow, crooked, obstructed, and shallow, that only the very smallest steamers, coal barges and tugs could make their way. The gunboats thus got far ahead, and the rebels, discovering this, placed obstructions not only in front of the gunboats, but in their rear, so as to cut them off from the troops. The sharpshooters of the enemy also annoyed Porter from the banks, and rebel artillery was placed at intervals. This threatened the absolute loss of the gunboat fleet, and Porter sent back for Sherman to hurry to his rescue. Sherman got the news at night, but started at once along a narrow strip of dry land which fortunately existed here, led his troops by lighted candles through the canebrake, and drove away the rebel assailants. Then, though with infinite difficulty, the obstructions in the rear were removed, and the gunboats set about returning; there was not room to turn, and they had to back out for miles; but on the 27th of March the unsuccessful expedition was back in front of Vicksburg.

Meanwhile, Grant had other enemies to contend with besides the rebels and the elements. There were constant efforts being made to supersede him. McClernand was still manœuvring to obtain command of the expedition, and was constantly annoying Grant by his insubordination and inefficiency, yet Grant was not allowed to remove him. The country was dissatisfied with the lack of success, and the Government was impatient. But although of course all these things were harassing in the extreme, Grant did not allow them to interfere with his determination or his energy. So long as he was continued in command, he would intermit no exertion; but it was painful indeed to feel that he was losing the confidence of the country and the Government, through the machinations of inefficient rivals and political subordinates, at a time when he needed all the moral support that could be bestowed. The rebels laughed with exultant glee at his baffled schemes, and their partisans at the North taunted him with his failures and his slowness. But all this while he never doubted that he should achieve success, and never failed to express this confidence to his superiors and to his own command, infusing into the latter, at least, some of the spirit that animated and encouraged him.

EAST OF VICKSBURG.

Every plan to reach Vicksburg by water having failed, Grant finally devised another, which depended upon the subsidence of the floods.

It was now April, and before long the overflow must begin to abate in some degree. He proposed to make use of a system of bayous starting from near the Mississippi, opposite the mouth of the Yazoo, and running to a point below Vicksburg, on the western shore. By this route the supplies and artillery were to be transported on steamers, while the troops could march by land. When they should arrive below, Grant was ordered to send a corps to Banks, who was now in New Orleans with a large army, about to attack Port Hudson, the only other fort yet held by the rebels on the Mississippi. After Por' Hudson should be taken, the plan was for Banks to come up and coöperate with Grant in the attack on Vicksburg.

But Grant's best officers opposed this plan. Those in whose judgment and fidelity he had most confidence implored him not to risk the inevitable dangers of such a campaign. Sherman especially urged him, in conversation and in writing, not to undertake it. This scheme would separate the army entirely from its base; Vicksburg would be between Grant and the Government, and all his supplies. The hazard was prodigious, for failure was utter ruin; defeat was annihilation. Grant knew this well, but his confidence was absolute, both in his army and in himself; and although he asserted neither with enthusiasm, he was tenacious in his resolve. He heard all the arguments with patience and consideration, but they did not move him a particle. He felt that the temper of the country was despondent; no success had occurred for many weary months; it was necessary to revive its spirit. To make a retrograde movement, as Sherman proposed, would elate the rebels and depress his own troops, while it would have a disastrous effect upon the courage of the North. Besides which, Grant felt certain that he should be victorious in this new campaign; and though he noted all the dangers, he calmly determined to incur them.

The orders for the movement were issued, and from that moment Sherman's opposition ceased. He worked as hard thereafter to insure success as he had striven before to prevent the campaign. The movement was begun on the 2d of March. The roads were intolerably bad; bridges were broken, streams overflowed, the results of the long inundation made the mud deep, and the troops plodded and plunged along. When they reached the point where they were to strike the Mississippi, below Vicksburg, the levee was found to be broken, and they had to be ferried for two miles; but the labor and time consumed in moving an entire army with all its stores in small boats, was so great, that a detour was made instead to a point lower down the river, making the entire distance to march, from the point of starting, seventy miles. Just at this juncture, the river fell, and the streams by which Grant expected to move his artillery and supplies became unnavigable, so that all the heavy ordnance and commissary stores had to be hauled along the miserable muddy roads.

This could not possibly be accomplished in months; and to obviate the new difficulty, Grant now proposed a daring scheme to the naval commander, who had been his able and faithful coadjutor in all these efforts. Grant was to run three steamers and ten barges by the Vicksburg batteries, while seven of Porter's iron-clads should engage the rebels, covering the passage of the unarmed vessels. Porter agreed, and on the 16th of April the attempt was made. It was a dark night, and the gunboats led the way. Soon, however, the rebels set fire to houses on the shore, and thus got light to direct their guns on the passing fleet. The storm of missiles was terrific; every vessel was struck, several were disabled, and one took fire, burning to the water's edge. The gunboats fought the batteries manfully, and for two hours and forty minutes this wonderful midnight battle raged. All the population of Vicksburg came out to witness it, and the Union troops, in their distant camps, were also spectators of the scene. But, with a single exception, every transport and gunboat passed the ordeal; only eight men were wounded, and the Henry Clay was the only vessel destroyed.

This part of the enterprise was so successful, that ten days afterwards, six other transports and twelve barges made a similar attempt; one transport was sunk, but half of the barges got safely by, so that Grant now had a good supply of provisions below Vicksburg, and Porter's seven gunboats were also there for use in any further movements. Two corps of troops had meanwhile arrived by land, and on the 29th of April a gunboat-attack was made, at Grant's request, on a formidable work on the eastern shore, called Grand Gulf. This place was in reality an outwork of Vicksburg; although fifty miles below the town, it was at the first point where there was any hard land on which troops could be landed. The hills here are as precipitous as at Vicksburg, and thirteen heavy guns were mounted. A gallant attempt by Porter to silence these guns was made, but failed. Grant had his troops on transports ready to land them, the moment the batteries were silenced; and when the impossibility of this was discovered, he immediately went aboard Porter's flag-ship and asked him once more to run his iron-clads by the batteries.

4

So prompt was his decision.* As soon as one effort failed he had another to try, and not waiting to deliberate, he put it at once into execution, leaving the rebels no time to recover from the effect of the first attack, before they must reply to the second. This wonderful faculty of deciding promptly at the critical moment, of retaining his heart amid what seemed irrevocable or absolute defeat, and still more the ability to direct, and the courage and judgment to order, at a crisis, no man ever possessed in a more remarkable degree. At such times, Grant's head is always clearest; immediately after a seeming repulse, his courage mounts highest; in the thickest gloom of what to any one else would be irremediable disaster, his genius is most fertile, his judgment most prompt and excellent, his action most decided.

The night after the defeat before Grand Gulf, he landed his troops again on the western shore, and marched them to a point below that work, and out of the reach of its guns. Meanwhile the transports ran by the batteries, while Porter again engaged the enemy, and then himself passed below with his gunboats. During the morning, the Thirteenth corps was once more embarked on the steamers. Reconnoissances of the eastern shore had developed the fact that there was little hard land even yet on that bank; but in the night, a negro brought information of a good road leading from a place called Bruinsburg, six miles below Grand Gulf, up to high ground in the interior. To Bruinsburg, therefore, Grant moved with his advance.

Meanwhile, Sherman had been ordered to remain above, and make an attack on the north of Vicksburg, merely to distract the attention of the enemy from the important movements on the southern side. In this he was assisted by the gunboat force left there by Porter, and on the 29th and 30th, a formidable demonstration succeeded in alarming and occupying the garrison at Vicksburg. Grant had been very unwilling to order this demonstration, because Sherman had already suffered unjustly in the estimation of the country from his former failure in front of Vicksburg. He told Sherman of this unwillingness, and the latter replied: "I believe a diversion at Haine's Bluff is proper and right, and will make it, let whatever reports of repulses be made." The magnanimity evinced in this instance by both these great soldiers, was conspicuous again and again during their career. Grant constantly sought to advance and promote his friend, shielding him from unmerited obloquy, and affording him opportunities to make an independent fame; while Sherman steadily supported his chief, never seeking to supplant him nor assuming to rival him. Each by this marvellously unselfish conduct, not only added a new lustre to his own reputation, but did good service to the cause for which each was contending. Grant thus secured the complete execution of his own great plans, while Sherman received the assistance of his friend, who never climbed a step on the ladder of promotion, without reaching a hand to help up the distinguished soldier who was just behind. No more admirable instance of heroic friendship can be found in the history of war. Happy the Republic whose institutions develop such characters, and whose greatest men throw such a reflex lustre on the institutions which produced them!

Before beginning his march on the western bank, Grant had given orders for a cavalry movement into the interior of Mississippi, under Colonel Grierson. This was to start from the northern boundary of the State, to destroy bridges, cut railroads, and, avoiding large forces of the enemy, to do all the damage possible to the rebel communications, isolating the garrison of Vicksburg, and alarming the inhabitants of the entire State; for the whole population of the South was now at war. There were no able-bodied men out of the rebel service; those who were not in the regular army were spies and partisans, and Grant in his turn determined to make war upon the *people* as well as upon the *armies* of the South. His orders were constant *not to molest or injure women or children; not to do damage to property without some military object;* but he deliberately sought to destroy all the military resources of the rebellion. Among these, none were more important than supplies of food. The rebel armies were kept up by means of the subsistence stores forwarded to them from the interior, and Grant began now the plan of destroying those stores, just as he would arms or ammunition. The rebels themselves chose that the war should be a partisan one, and Grant accepted the situation; he fought the people as well as the armies of the enemy, *and he conquered them all.*

This raid of Grierson's was eminently successful. It was the first of those great expeditions which, penetrating into distant regions that fancied themselves secure, brought home the punishment of rebellion to the quietest hamlets; which carried destruction to the very source and root of rebel strength; and, when combined with more terrible attacks on the rebel armies at the front, finally produced the result at which the nation was aiming. For, while Grant always chose to do himself the hardest fighting, he sent one after another of his subordinates upon expeditions of this character, sometimes with regiments, sometimes with armies, into the interior of the so-called Confederacy. He held the monster by the throat, and sent others to give stabs to the unprotected vitals, till finally Rebellion fell. Grierson made a march of six hundred miles in sixteen days, producing as much moral as purely military effect, and at the most opportune moment for Grant's great campaign.

The Thirteenth corps, under McClernand, had the advance in crossing the Mississippi; after them came two divisions of the Seventeenth, under McPherson. These were all landed at Bruinsburg, on the eastern shore, during the 30th of April. They were supplied with three days' rations, which they were ordered to make last five. Neither tents nor baggage was taken; no personal effects, even for officers, were ferried across until all the troops were over. Grant took not even his own horse, but borrowed one on the road from a soldier. Everything now depended on rapidity of motion, and Admiral Porter loaned his gunboats to ferry artillery and troops.

A road leads direct from the landing to the bluffs, a mile or two distant, and the men were pushed on at once in the direction of Port Gibson, a town at the junction of the road from Bruinsburg with another leading to Grand Gulf. The direct road leads to Jackson, the capital of the State, fifty miles to the northwest. It was important to seize Port Gibson at once, so as to hold these various roads. The possession of this place secured Grand Gulf, which would be cut off entirely whenever Port Gibson fell. During the night, McClernand's advance came in contact with the rebels a few miles from the town, the garrison of Grand Gulf having marched promptly out to oppose the movement of Grant. At daylight the battle began. The rebels were about eleven thousand strong; Grant heard the firing at the Landing, and started at once for the front, arriving at ten o'clock. The battle was even for several hours, the rebels having great advantages of position, but about noon McPherson's corps arrived, giving Grant the superiority in numbers; he at once threw fresh troops both to the right and left of McClernand, and before night the position was completely turned, and the enemy driven in confusion to Port Gibson. The ground was very rugged, and completely unknown to the Union army, so that Grant was obliged to delay the pursuit until daylight, when, on pushing into the town, it was found to be evacuated. In this battle Grant had about nineteen thousand men engaged; he lost over eight hundred men killed and wounded, and took six hundred and fifty prisoners, besides killing and wounding more than as many of

the enemy. His success was due entirely to the celerity and unexpected character of his movements. The enemy was admirably posted
on a steep ridge, protected by a broken country covered with tangled
vine and underbrush, and the rebels fought well. Reinforcements of
five thousand men had been ordered from Vicksburg and others from
Jackson, but they only arrived in time to share the flight.

In their retreat, they burnt the bridges over several streams, and
Grant next day was obliged to rebuild these, before he could make
any progress. But extraordinary efforts were made, the houses in the
neighborhood were torn down for timber, and officers and men worked
up to their waists in the water. In one instance, the troops arrived
at a bridge while it was still burning, and extinguished the fire. The
two corps were pushed on, that day and the next, about fifteen
miles, to the Big Black river, skirmishing with the enemy all the way.
But Grand Gulf was now uncovered, and Grant himself rode off in
that direction with a small escort. He found the town already in
possession of the naval forces, which had landed early in the day.
The rebels had not been able to save their heavy cannon, and thirteen
pieces fell into the hands of the victors.

Grant had not been undressed since crossing the river, three days
before, and now went aboard the gunboats, where he borrowed a shirt,
and wrote dispatches nearly all night. He ordered Sherman to move
down on the opposite side of the river and join the main army ; he
informed the Government of his own movements, and gave orders to
his subordinates to forward supplies as rapidly as possible. All his
supplies, of every description, had to come seventy miles by land on
the western bank, then to be ferried across to Bruinsburg, and so
moved up to the army. Upon everybody he urged the overwhelming
importance of celerity ; for as soon as the enemy should become aware
that the whole Union army was on the eastern bank, of course every
possible effort would be made to destroy it.

At Grand Gulf, Grant got word from Banks that changed the whole
character of his campaign. Heretofore he had intended to march to
Port Hudson, several hundred miles, and to join Banks in the attack
on that place; and when this was over, both armies were to move up
against Vicksburg. But Banks now sent him word that he could not
be at Port Hudson before the 10th of May, and even after Port Hudson had fallen, he could not march to Vicksburg with more than twelve
thousand men. This information decided Grant not to go to Banks
at all. He would lose more than twelve thousand men on the march

to Port Hudson, and in the siege and probable battles there; so that he would be no stronger on his return than now. Besides this, he had already won a victory; he had got his army on dry ground, where he had been striving all winter to place it; he had captured Grand Gulf, and was on the high road to Vicksburg or Jackson. He felt the importance of seizing these advantages, and of making the most of the moral effects of his triumph, both with his own troops and with the enemy. He made up his mind that night to commence the Vicksburg campaign. It was fortunate indeed for the country that Banks sent him the message of delay.

Vicksburg now was only twenty miles off, with one large river, the Big Black, in the way. It was defended by fifty-two thousand men, either in the garrison or in the interior of the State; this force was under Pemberton. Another but smaller rebel army at Jackson, fifty miles directly west from Vicksburg, was eventually commanded by Jo. Johnston; at this time it amounted to ten thousand or twelve thousand men, though before the campaign terminated it was quadrupled. To oppose these two formidable bodies of troops, Grant would have, when Sherman should arrive, not more than thirty-five thousand men in column, and twenty light batteries. The rebels had at least three hundred guns. They were also on the defensive, and in a country with every inch of which they were familiar, and where every inhabitant was their friend, their partisan, their spy. The two rebel forces, if combined, would certainly largely outnumber, and perhaps crush the Union army. Instead, therefore, of moving at once against Vicksburg, Grant determined to push directly between the two hostile forces, separate them completely, and attack the smaller one before the other could come to the rescue; to drive it east as far as Jackson, where all the railroads centre by which Vicksburg was supplied; and after destroying Johnston, and the rebel stores and communications at Jackson, to return and capture Vicksburg at his leisure.

No more daring enterprise was ever undertaken in war. To perform it, he must abandon his base of supplies entirely; for, if he moved east after Johnston, Pemberton would be sure to fall upon his line of communications in rear; and to guard this line would weaken Grant, so that he could not be strong enough for the operations he contemplated. He therefore sent word to have the greatest possible amount of supplies forwarded him before starting, and determined to cut loose entirely from his base, depending on the country for all further rations and forage. A parallel feat had then never been performed with a modern army. He gave no notice of his intention to the Government in advance, and it was lucky that he did not, for as soon as Halleck discovered the plan, he sent word to Grant to return; but it was too late; the order did not reach Grant till the campaign was decided.

Sherman was hurried up, the greatest possible energy inculcated upon everybody, dispositions made of the troops which were to remain on the west side of the Mississippi and at Grand Gulf, and, on the 7th of May the venturous column started for Jackson. Meanwhile, Grant's horses had arrived and his mess furniture. Hitherto he had depended on the hospitality of his subordinates, not only for a horse, but for every meal of the campaign. Sherman's corps arrived just as the advance of the army was starting; and he was directed by Grant to take *three days' rations for men, and make them last seven.* On the 11th, Grant informed Halleck, *"As I shall communicate with Grand Gulf no more, you may not hear from me again for several days."* This was the very day on which Halleck sent word to Grant to return and coöperate with Banks. The two dispatches crossed each other on the way; but there was no telegraph communication, and each was a week in reaching its destination.

The army moved northeast, on different but neighboring roads, meeting no enemy in force until the 12th, when McPherson, who had the advance on the right, fell in with a body of rebels five thousand strong, at a place called Raymond. The main rebel force, under Pemberton, was on the left, at Edwards's Station, on the railroad between Vicksburg and Jackson. Grant disposed his forces so as to threaten Pemberton, and induced that commander to remain in mass awaiting an attack; Pemberton at the same time sent word for the troops at Jackson to come out and assault Grant's rear. But Grant, instead of attacking Pemberton, where the rebels were prepared in force, sent McPherson, with a whole corps, to overwhelm the smaller force coming up from Jackson. McPherson met the rebels at Raymond, and, outnumbering them two to one, completely routed them, and occupied the town. This was the second victory of the campaign, and the second time that Grant, with a force not half so large as that of the rebels combined, was able, by the wisdom of his combinations and the celerity of his movements, to divide and beat his enemy in detail. Meanwhile Pemberton had been expecting the attack at Edwards's Station. From Raymond, the rebels fled at once to Jackson, and with one of those opportune decisions which come only to masters in war at the critical moment, Grant instantly changed his plans. Hitherto he had meant to send only one corps to Jackson; but this day's fight confirmed him in the idea that a large force was on his right, and it was necessary to dispose of this effectually, so that when he turned towards Vicksburg, he should leave no formidable enemy in his rear. Large rebel reinforcements were hastening to Jackson, and he determined to destroy the troops already there before the reinforcements should arrive in great numbers. That night he issued orders for the three corps to start for Jackson; and on the 13th this was done at dawn, McPherson and Sherman having the advance, on separate roads; and McClernand following each. The same night, General Jo. Johnston arrived at Jackson, and took command of all the rebels in the State. He at once sent orders for Pemberton to come up in Grant's rear and attack the national troops, meaning with the garrison of Jackson to coöperate in front, and thus crush Grant, as between the upper and the nether millstone.

This was a very good plan, but Johnston had Grant to deal with, who knew the danger of such a movement as Johnston ordered. Grant too was never slow. He now moved his troops with great rapidity, and on the 14th, Sherman and McPherson were in front of Jackson, while Pemberton had not yet left Edwards's Station, twenty miles away.

The attack was begun by McPherson at 11 o'clock, and fighting lasted three hours, during which McPherson drove the rebels inside their works. Sherman was moving up on the right and south of Jackson, Grant being with this portion of his army. Some obstacles in front seemed important, and Grant rode to the extreme right in person, to reconnoitre, when he found that the enemy had evacuated the town; he rode on, and his party was with the first to enter Jackson. The rebels had made all their resistance in McPherson's front, and, finding that Pemberton had not come up to the assault, finally withdrew, while Sherman was reconnoitring and getting into position. By three o'clock, the two corps were in Jackson, Johnston retreating out of the north side of the town. Seventeen cannon were captured, and the enemy lost eight hundred and forty-five men in killed, wounded, and prisoners. Grant's entire loss was less than three hundred.

Grant had now attained the object of his eastward march. It was important at once to destroy the railroads and stores of the rebels, and, in order to effect this, he was obliged to abandon or postpone any pursuit of Johnston. Twenty miles of railroad were accordingly torn up, and the bridges burnt; all the rebel supplies, factories, and arsenals were included in the conflagration. That night Grant slept in the quarters occupied the day before by Johnston. The reinforcements that were coming up to the enemy were obliged to make wide and long detours to join their commander. But, although success had been so marked, it was still not complete. There was yet imminent danger of a concentration of the two rebel armies; and before night, Grant got possession of a dispatch from Johnston to Pemberton, directing the concentration so much to be feared.

He determined to prevent this, and accordingly, with his usual promptitude, he that afternoon ordered McPherson to retrace his steps, marching in the morning in the direction of Edwards's Station. McClernand was also informed of the defeat of Johnston, and of the danger of rebel concentration. His troops were at once faced about in the same direction as McPherson's. The various corps were admirably located, so as to converge on the same point, which was Bolton, a station a few miles east of Edwards's, where Pemberton was known to be. The men were fatigued, having been marching or fighting incessantly since the 7th, but there was no time now for rest. Celerity of movement won battles and saved lives. Accordingly, early on the morning of the 15th, the two corps had turned their faces towards Vicksburg, and were in motion for the enemy. Sherman was to spend that day destroying the munitions and military resources in and around Jackson. Before night, McPherson and McClernand were within supporting distance of each other at Bolton, and ordered to march in the morning for Edwards's Station; while Pemberton still delayed, in disobedience of Johnston's orders. He did not dream that Grant had no communications with the Mississippi, and his idea was to march south and cut those communications. On the morning of the 15th, he moved for this purpose southeast of Edwards's Station, away from Johnston, who had by this time been driven north from Jackson, so that the rebels were actually moving in opposite directions, while Grant was converging between them; Pemberton striving to cut Grant's communications with the Mississippi, while Grant, who had cut them himself nine days before, was returning to Vicksburg, and seeking Pemberton to destroy him.

Pemberton moved slowly, and again received positive orders from Johnston to join him. On the 16th, he finally concluded to obey, and reversed his column. But in the night Grant had got word of Pemberton's exact force and position, and of the design to attack the national rear. He instantly dispatched to Sherman to start at once from Jackson to the support of the main army. "The fight may be brought on at any moment; *we should have every man on the field.*" A national division was now coming up alone from Grand Gulf, and this was also ordered to join the main army. "Pass your troops to the front of your trains, and *keep the ammunition in front of all others.*" He meant work.

Three roads lead to Edwards's Station from the east, and on the northern one Grant had four divisions, under McPherson, while on each of the others were two divisions; all these last under McClernand. Sherman had not got up. The advance of McClernand encountered Pemberton's skirmishers just as the reverse movement of the rebel column began, and the enemy at once fell into an admirable position, covering all three roads. The rebel left was on a hill called Champion's Hill, and by eleven o'clock the force under McPherson assaulted here. Grant was with this portion of his command in person. The rebels had twenty-five thousand men, a defensive position, and, as usual, complete knowledge of the country, of which, of course, the national troops were entirely ignorant. The battle raged with various fortune for several hours; the Union soldiers gained a point on the hill several times, but were driven back as often, and Grant sent repeated orders to McClernand to come up to the support; but that commander allowed an inferior force to amuse and delay him, and, in spite of Grant's positive directions to attack, he did not obey. Finally, Grant sent troops to the extreme rebel left and rear, and these produced such an effect that, combined with another direct attack in front, the enemy gave way, and the hill was carried, McClernand not having been engaged at all. One of his divisions had been on the right with Grant all day, and in the thickest of the fight, but those under McClernand's direct command were not in the battle.

The rout of the rebels was complete, and as McClernand now came up in force, Grant sent these fresh troops in pursuit. Grant had not had more than fifteen thousand men engaged. He lost about two thousand four hundred men in the battle of Champion's Hill, which was by far the hardest fought in the whole campaign. The enemy's loss was between three thousand and four thousand killed and wounded, and as many more prisoners, besides thirty cannon. In addition to this, one whole division was cut off from the bulk of the rebel army in the precipitous flight. It struggled along, making a wide detour, and reported to Johnston several days afterwards, but Pemberton never com-

manded it again.   The moral effects of this victory were prodigious.
The rebel troops broke and fled in every direction ; artillerymen deserted their guns in the retreat, and many of the soldiers threw away
their small arms, and gave themselves up prisoners before they were
asked.   The pursuit was continued till after dark, reaching fifteen
miles.   Grant himself was with the advance, and his party got so far
ahead of the main column, that they were obliged to return to a more
secure position for the night.   That night Grant received Halleck's
orders to return to the Mississippi and coöperate with Banks; but the,
best way to return now was to proceed in his career of victory.

It was nothing but the marvellous energy and promptness of Grant
that won this battle.   Pemberton was actually moving to join Johnston when he was struck by Grant; had the national commander delayed a day, the concentration would have been effected; but it was
now forever impossible.

The next day the pursuit was pushed on ; Sherman having arrived
at Bolton by the close of the 15th, he was ordered to move at once to
the right of the rest of the command.   Grant reached the Big Black
river, the only one now between his army and Vicksburg, early in the
morning of the 17th, his advance having started before daylight.   At
the crossing of the railroad over this river, the rebels had established
a formidable work; here the river makes a bend like a horse-shoe,
open towards the east, and the line of fortifications was across this
opening, reaching from the river above to the river again below.   The
ground in front was swampy and exposed to the rebel fire, while still
beyond, on the western bank of the river, rose steep bluffs, commanding the country for miles.   This point was defended by twenty cannon
and four thousand troops, who ought to have held it against direct
assault forever.   But the Union troops were inspired by the long
series of successes, and the rebels were exhausted with disaster and
retreat.   At the first attack, by only about eleven hundred men, the
rebels fled in dismay, abandoning all their guns, and only seeking to
reach the river.   The panic spread to the troops on the opposite shore,
who set fire to the bridge, and nearly eighteen hundred prisoners, with
eighteen pieces of artillery, were captured.   Grant lost only two hundred and fifty men, of whom but twenty-nine were killed.   This of
course was only the result of the rout of the day before, for the rebels
had often and often proved themselves good enough soldiers.

But their depression now was terrible.   Many left their ranks, and
vowed they would surrender rather than fight again under Pemberton.
The people of the country joined them, and all fled pell mell into

Vicksburg, from the conqueror who had won five battles in less than twenty days, captured six thousand five hundred of the enemy, and killed and wounded six thousand more. He had done this, after starting with an average of two days' rations, and he had subsisted his own army, besides beating two of the enemy's, and lost only seven hundred killed and three thousand four hundred wounded.

After rebuilding the bridges out of the wood of houses torn down for the purpose, he pressed rapidly on, and on the 18th of May Vicksburg was besieged. No more brilliant series of operations is chronicled in the history of war. For originality of conception, for daring in execution, for admirable combinations, for strategical foresight, for promptness in the decisions and celerity in the movements, for completeness of success in each operation, and for the magnificent result of all, they have no parallel except in the achievements of Napoleon.

SIEGE OF VICKSBURG.

The country around Vicksburg is broken and difficult in an extraordinary degree; full of rough hills and rougher ravines, with numerous creeks running between the various heights, and a thick growth of underbrush or forest covering the sides of the cliffs and chasms; a region expressly adapted for defence. These natural advantages had been developed to their utmost by the rebels, whose line of works, located on the most salient ridges, reached entirely around the city. Numerous detached forts were built at intervals, and between these stretched an uninterrupted line of rifle-pits, not less than eight miles long. Outside of the parapet, the enemy had formed an unusually difficult abatis of fallen trees. Within these lines, Pemberton had now nearly thirty-five thousand men, for he was of course reinforced by the garrison proper, of the town. A hundred guns at least were also ready to repel assault. Johnston, however, feared that even with all these defences, natural and artificial, Pemberton would finally be compelled to surrender; he therefore ordered his subordinate to evacuate the place. But again Grant's promptness intervened to frustrate the plans of his antagonist. Pemberton held a council of war on the 18th of May, and while it was still deliberating, Grant took his position on the outside and invested Vicksburg. The Union line at first was incomplete. Sherman had the right, McPherson the centre, and McClernand at this time the extreme left; but the troops of the last-named officer did not extend to the Mississippi; while Sherman's right rested on the very hills from which he had been repelled in January before.

Grant did not delay operations, but the day after arriving before the town, he ordered an assault. With his usual tactics, he wished to take advantage of the demoralization of the rebels, before they had time to recover. Accordingly, on the 19th of May, all three of his corps commanders were instructed to charge against the rebel line; but the sight of the rebel fastness, these lofty hills shutting in Vicksburg on every hand, these hundred cannon directed against the assailants, the reinforcements of eight thousand men in garrison, and the knowledge of the extraordinary difficulties Grant must overcome before he could carry the works, so strong by nature and by art, reanimated the defenders. The corps of Sherman and of McPherson pushed up close to the rebel works, but neither was able to make an impression; and McClernand, whose troops were further from the city than either of the others, did not get up in time to really participate in the assault. The effort was therefore unsuccessful; no entrance was gained; but positions close to the enemy were obtained and held, which proved of vast importance during the siege. The prodigious difficulties before them had not been known to the besiegers until now, and it was evident that even all the battles and victories they had won had not achieved the consummation at which for so many months they had been aiming.

Grant now spent two days in resting his troops after the wonderful campaign through which they had passed; in bringing up supplies, from the new base which was established on the Yazoo; and in preparing for a second and more determined assault; for he was loath to begin the tedious processes of a siege. His men, exhilarated by the success of the brilliant campaign, were also unlikely to set to work in in the trenches with zeal until they knew that no other means would even yet suffice to conquer Vicksburg. After their successes at Champion's Hill and the Big Black, they thought themselves irresistible. Besides this, Johnston's army, still near Jackson, was daily receiving reinforcements, and would soon, perhaps, equal Grant's in numbers, and be able to raise the siege; while, if Grant could once secure possession of the town, with the river open for communication and supplies, the national forces could laugh to scorn any rebel attempt to regain it.

On the 22d of May, therefore, a second assault was ordered. It was preceded by a vigorous bombardment both from the fleet and from a line of a hundred cannon mounted along the hills in the interior. Precisely at ten, the various columns moved against the rebel works.

The attack was made with great vigor all along the line; the men moved by the roads when this was practicable, and elsewhere down into the ravines and up the precipitous sides, on which the hostile fortifications awaited them. But the difficulties were insurmountable; the assailants were exposed for a distance of several hundred yards to the artillery and musketry fire of the besieged; they got entangled in the brushwood; they were shot down before they could scale the hills. Everywhere they were repelled; and although prodigies of valor had been performed, it was all in vain. Each corps had recoiled. The national flag in front of each had been planted on the rebel works, and still remained there, but the troops were unable to penetrate further, while the rebels dared not take the flags away. The battle was over, and no result was gained.

At this moment McClernand sent a dispatch to Grant, announcing the capture of two forts. This message was three times repeated, and Grant was urged to order another assault, to support the advantage said to have been gained by McClernand. Supposing that McClernand must know when a fort was gained, Grant complied with the request, and a second assault was ordered by Sherman's and McPherson's worn out men. This met with a similar result with the former one; the loss of life was nearly doubled, and no more success was attained; while it proved that McClernand had originally secured no advantage like that which he had proclaimed. He had carried no fort, and when the assault he requested was renewed solely to support him, he did not himself attain any advantage beyond what the others had already procured.

At night three thousand national soldiers had been killed or wounded; about thirty thousand had been engaged. Pemberton declared that he had eighteen thousand five hundred men in the trenches; he lost about one thousand soldiers in this fight. The disparity of course was occasioned by the rebels being under cover. Shortly after this assault, McClernand was relieved by General Ord, at the command of Grant.

The national troops, however, although repelled, were not discouraged, and their leader at once set about his preparations for a siege. These operations were unintermitted for over forty days. Reinforcements were sent to Grant in large numbers, his lines were rendered continuous, and were daily advanced further against the doomed city. Mines were dug and sprung, and the city was completely shut off from all supply or communication, except when an occasional rebel scout found his way through the Union lines. Meanwhile, Johnston also was reinforced, till his army amounted to forty thousand men, and moved up on Grant's rear to relieve the city. But Grant now commanded seventy thousand soldiers, half of whom he kept in the trenches, and the other half he formed into a corps of observation against Johnston. These built a line of works facing east, protecting the besiegers, who were thus enclosed between two lines—one in front and one in rear.

Towards the last of June the sufferings of the besieged became very great. They were forced to put the men on quarter rations, and finally, after it became apparent to Pemberton that all hope of rescue had disappeared; when it was certain that Johnston, with his forty thousand men, would not dare attack Grant in rear, although he would be supported by the entire garrison in front; when neither the siege could be raised nor the garrison escape; when the blockade by land and river was so effectual, that attempts to build boats and cross the Mississippi were detected; when scouts were intercepted, bringing word to Pemberton that Johnston could do no more for him, and from Pemberton, that his supplies of food and ammunition were both exhausted; when for forty-seven days the besiegers and besieged had lain in the hot trenches, working, digging, mining, countermining, assaulting, repelling, advancing, retreating, sickening, dying; those inside almost starving, those outside often suffering from lack of water; both sides exposed to miasma and heat, and rain, and fatigue, and incessant danger from bursting shells and sharpshooters' rifles, and sudden attacks by night and day—finally, the mighty siege was about to terminate.

All this while Grant's patience had never failed him. The country had long since become anxious and irritable; again, notwithstanding his brilliant series of victories, there had been talk of relieving him; but he remained calm and undisturbed. He had a mighty fortress, containing a hostile army, in his front, and another army at his rear, generaled by one of the greatest soldiers of the rebellion; his approaches were slow, his assaults had been repelled; his mines had produced no effect; the rebels seemed determined, his own men sickened and wearied under the protracted exposure of the trenches and the fatigues of night-work in this insalubrious climate; seven weeks had passed since he had returned from his career of triumphant battles, and still he was outside of the works which seven weeks before he thought he had gained. But his confidence of success remained undiminished; his energy never flagged. He met a rebel woman once, while making the circuit of his lines, who asked him, with a taunt, how long he expected to remain before Vicksburg; "I do not know how long I shall have to wait," he replied, "but *I shall stay here till I take the town, if it takes me thirty years.*" This was the spirit that animated him, and which he was able to infuse into his soldiers, who, despite all their toils, and hardships, and dangers, were as determined as he, and had no thought of abandoning the enterprise, which they had already done so much to accomplish. The spirit of their commander held officers and men steadily up to their tedious and unexciting task; this spirit finally conquered Vicksburg.

For, on the 3d of July, Pemberton made overtures to Grant, and the same day a meeting of the two generals was held between their lines, and in sight of both armies. It took place under an oak tree, which has since been cut down to furnish mementoes of the occasion. The troops for miles around hung over their parapets on either side, watching the interview on which the destinies of the two armies depended. But Pemberton was absurd and haughty, and refused the simple surrender which Grant demanded. In the night, however, he consulted with his subordinates, and came to a better mind. By morning, he had agreed to deliver up the garrison, with all its munitions, as prisoners of war. Grant did not wish the trouble of feeding another army, and could not, in many weeks, procure transports sufficient to send his prisoners North; he therefore stipulated that they should be paroled and sent into the interior, not to fight again until exchanged. Nearly the same terms which Napoleon granted to the Austrians at the famous surrender of Ulm.

On the 4th of July, therefore—auspicious anniversary—the capture was consummated. Grant generously allowed the officers to retain their swords, and both officers and men their private property; but the muskets were all stacked by the rebels themselves outside their works, between the lines. It took them nearly all day to march out of their defences, and lay down their colors and their arms, the national army looking on. *Thirty-two thousand rebel soldiers thus became prisoners to Grant;* over two thousand one hundred of these were officers, and among them no fewer than fifteen generals. *One hundred and seventy-two cannon also were surrendered. No such capture of men and material had been made before in modern times.* The greatest of Napoleon's triumphs pales before the achievement. General Halleck declared that the famous operations about Ulm were eclipsed by those which had secured this result; and the glowing pages of European historians, in recounting the magnificent success of the greatest of European soldiers, do not reach the points of pane-gyric which simple facts declare to have been won by Grant. At Ulm, Napoleon received the surrender of sixty pieces of cannon and thirty thousand men. At Vicksburg, our American hero became the master of one hundred and seventy-two hostile cannon, and thirty-two thousand prisoners.

It required an entire week to complete the paroles; but on the 11th of July the rebel garrison marched finally out of Vicksburg, never to return, except as submissive citizens of the United States. On the 8th, Port Hudson, the only other point held by the enemy on the Mis-sissipi, surrendered to General Banks; the rebel commander announ-cing that, as Vicksburg had fallen, he had no hope of relief, or of successfully enduring a siege. So that the great river was once more open in its entire length to the national flags, and the greatest bond that held the rebellion together was broken forever.

On the very day that Grant received propositions for Pemberton's surrender, he sent orders to Sherman to get his command in readiness to march against Johnston's army; and on the 4th, as soon as the capture of the town was really consummated, he sent Sherman in pursuit of the enemy outside. Johnston, however, fell back in haste, when he heard of the fall of Vicksburg, and a hot chase was made, Sherman following as far as Jackson; but thence Johnson escaped into the interior, Sherman not pursuing farther. Great destruction was again made of railroads and resources, at and around Jackson, and the undisturbed possession of the State of Mississippi was thus secured; Sherman then returned to Vicksburg, and the troops were allowed a month or two of rest, after their long labors in the trenches and the field.

Grant had now completely accomplished the Vicksburg campaign, one of the most brilliant recorded in history, whether its results are regarded, or the means by which those results were attained. He had fought five battles, made two assaults, and prosecuted a siege for forty-seven days and nights. He had captured an entire army, as well as the most difficult and important stronghold which the rebels then possessed in the whole theatre of war; he had opened the Missis-sippi river, *he had taken prisoner, killed, or wounded, over fifty thousand rebel soldiers, and captured two hundred and forty-six cannon,* during the campaign and siege. His own loss in the same time was one thou-

5

sand two hundred and forty-three killed, seven thousand and ninety-
five wounded, and five hundred and thirty-five missing; total, eight
thousand eight hundred and seventy-three. Of the wounded, more
than half returned to duty, many of them almost immediately.

The character of this campaign forever stamps the man who conceived and executed it, not only as a soldier of uncommon genius, but
as one of those great intellects which arise only once or twice in a
century. The magnificent daring of the original idea; its unlike-
ness to anything that had been done or planned during a generation;
the unflinching determination with which it was begun, despite the
discouragement and opposition of subordinates and superiors; the
moral courage which was required for this, at a moment when the fate
of the country almost hung on Grant's success, and his own downfall
was the certain consequence of disaster—the promptitude and the
unerring sagacity of the numerous and incalculably important decisions; the marvellous fertility of resources, and the equally marvellous
energy with which those resources were all brought into play; the
beautiful accuracy of the strategic combinations; the vigor of each
separate movement; the wisdom with which the plans of the enemy
were divined, and opposed by still more skillful ones; the unity with
which the various forces were made to act; the art with which they
were separated when necessary, yet always kept so that they could be
brought together at a critical moment; and the administrative ability
which moved, and supplied, and marched, and fought the army with
rapidity, daring, and unparalleled success—these are traits that no soldier of our time has possessed, in an equal degree, and characteristics
that in no time have been displayed by soldier or statesman without
placing their owner in the front rank for intellect and moral power.

Honors, of course, were heaped upon Grant after this unprecedented
triumph. He was made a major general in the regular army; the
President and the general-in-chief each wrote him letters of congratu-
lation; the legislatures of various States passed resolutions of thanks;
swords were presented him; and his name passed to the head of
all the defenders of the Union. His equanimity was as great, however, in success as it had been in disaster. He felt that there was still
other work to do, and at once asked permission to make a movement
against Mobile. But this was not allowed; and, instead, a corps of his
army was taken from him and given to Banks. He felt, however,
that his subordinates had worked hard to achieve the victories which
his abilities had planned, and one of his first efforts was to secure pro-

motion for them. A long list, headed by Sherman and McPherson, was made out, and nearly every one of his recommendations was approved. In August, he went to New Orleans, to consult with Banks about a combined movement against Mobile, which he still hoped he could persuade the Government to allow; and while there, he was thrown from his horse at a review, and received a hurt that lamed him for months. For twenty days he was confined to one position, and while thus suffering, word came to him of great apprehensions felt by the Government for the safety of the Union army at Chattanooga.

CHATTANOOGA.

This place, on the confines of Tennessee and Northern Georgia, and shut in by the Cumberland mountains and the Tennessee river, is at the junction of two great railroads, one passing north and south, the other east and west. It was parallel in military importance to Corinth, farther west; and, since the beginning of the war, the efforts of national commanders had been directed to secure its possession. If this were obtained, Richmond, the rebel capital, was cut off from all direct communication with the centre and west of the rebellious region. In September, by a series of masterly movements, Rosecranz succeeded in driving the rebel army that defended Chattanooga a few miles south of it, and himself stepped in to occupy the town. But it was certain that the rebels would make a prodigious effort to regain the prize, and Grant was directed to send all his available force to the support of Rosecranz.

Grant did not get these orders until his return from New Orleans, and, though still confined to his bed, at once dispatched a whole corps, under Sherman, towards Chattanooga. All expedition was made for the movement, but the distance was nearly a thousand miles, by the shortest route; half of this was by the river, and transports had to be procured; then there were four hundred miles to be marched through a hostile country. Long before Sherman could reach Rosecranz, the latter had been attacked by a superior force and driven into Chattanooga. The Government became greatly alarmed, and at once sent for Grant to take command of Rosecranz's army. He started, still a cripple, sailed up the Mississippi to Cairo, and then went by rail to Louisville; on the way he met the Secretary of War, and received from him an order placing him in command of all the armies west of the Alleghanies, except those of Banks, in Louisiana and Texas. His immediate task was to secure Chattanooga and the army there, which was now besieged, and to relieve East Tennessee, where Burnside also was in great straits, in command of another and smaller army.

Government had begun to perceive the necessity of concentrating its forces, and of having some unity in its military operations. Hitherto, the armies had acted each on its own plan, independent of every other, and often in contradictory directions. No one had been found able to combine the various resources and compel the different forces to coöperate. In this emergency, Grant, the only soldier who had met with continuous or brilliant success during the entire war, was called upon.

He had now absolute command of two hundred thousand men; but these were widely separated. He had a territory reaching from the Alleghanies to the Mississippi to hold and to guard, and large hostile armies to intercept and overthrow. At Chattanooga, the army which Rosecranz had commanded was crowded into a small area south of the Tennessee, and encircled by mountains, on which the rebels, so lately victorious, were encamped; there was but one railroad line of communication with this town, and that the enemy had just cut off; so that the solitary route by which all supplies could reach Chattanooga was a rugged mountain road, seventy miles long, and now almost impassable on account of heavy rains. The army was on half rations; ten thousand mules and horses had died of starvation, and there seemed no possibility of rescue. Burnside was two hundred miles away, in East Tennessee, equally isolated, though not besieged; and Sherman was in Mississippi, with four hundred miles to march before he could relieve Chattanooga; and even when he reached that place, unless the enemy were driven away, he would only add to the miseries of the Union troops, as those already there could not be supplied with either food or ammunition. This was the condition of affairs when Grant assumed his new command.

His first act was to place General George H. Thomas in the position lately occupied by Rosecranz. Grant assumed command on the 19th of October, but could not reach Chattanooga, on account of the break in communication, until the 23d. He telegraphed Thomas, however, on the 19th: "Hold Chattanooga at all hazards;" and Thomas replied, "I will hold the town till we starve." Grant went as far as Bridgeport by rail, and then took horse over the muddy mountain road. The rain fell in torrents, and often made it impossible for riders to keep their seats on the precipitous mountain sides. Grant was still lame from his fall, and had to be carried over such places in the arms of his soldiers; but all along the route he was dispatching directions to Thomas, ordering supplies of ordnance and provisions from the rear, or sending messages to Burnside and to Sherman, encouraging one and hastening the other.

He reached Chattanooga after dark, and that night was spent in looking over maps and studying the situation, apparently the gloomiest one in which a commander could be placed. The town is on the south side of the Tennessee, here very circuitous; the hills in front, not three miles off, called Missionary Ridge, were held by the enemy, whose line encircled Chattanooga, the rebel pickets reaching on both sides to the river. On Grant's right, the railroad runs west for a while and then north, to Nashville; but Lookout Mountain, two thousand two hundred feet high, was in the hands of the rebels, and completely commanded this railroad. Indeed, from the top of the mountain, the enemy easily threw shells into Chattanooga. The rebel army was greatly larger than Grant's, and elated with its victory, while the Union troops, cooped up among the hills, with a river at their back and no apparent means of rescue or escape, starving and nearly out of ammunition, seemed only waiting till the enemy should choose to demand surrender. The situation was quite as desperate as Pemberton's, on the 3d of July, at Vicksburg, for it was quite impossible to get the Union army away through the mountains on the north side of the Tennessee. But Pemberton was not in command at Chattanooga. *It was Grant.*

Next morning he made a reconnoissance of the country in the neighborhood of Lookout Mountain, and immediately gave directions for an aggressive movement in that direction. Portions of two corps from the army of the Potomac had been sent by Halleck to relieve Rosecranz, some weeks before; but these were still at Bridgeport, sixty miles away to the west, as their presence at Chattanooga would only serve to enhance the difficulties of supply. But Grant directed these troops, under Hooker, to move up to the western side of Lookout Mountain, which is only a mile or two in width, and at the same time ordered a coöperative movement from Chattanooga. Troops were sent on the night of the 27th, in boats, down the Tennessee, who eluded the rebel pickets, till they reached a point called Brown's ferry, on the south side of the river, some nine miles below the town. Here they landed, seized the ferry, drove in or captured the enemy's outguards, and maintained themselves while a bridge was laid, and a considerable force, that had been sent on the north side of the river, could be moved across the bridge. By ten o'clock, on the 28th, the position was secured. On the morning of the 26th, Hooker had moved from Bridgeport, and at six on the evening of the 28th he had marched around the foot of Lookout Mountain without serious opposition, secured the railroad, and connected with the force at Brown's Ferry.

The rebels, however, at once saw how important it was that this connection should be broken; for, if Grant was able to maintain it, his railroad communication would be open again with the north, and supplies of men, ammunition, and provisions could be sent him. Accordingly, that night they attacked Hooker in force, and a severe battle ensued, the result of which was that the enemy was driven off in confusion, and the railroad secured to Grant. The Union troops lost over four hundred men in killed and wounded, but the price was not too great to pay, for it secured the army in Chattanooga. Thus, in five days after Grant's arrival, the railroad to Nashville was opened, and the immediate danger repelled. Bragg, indeed, was now on the defensive, not Grant; for Hooker's position threatened Lookout Mountain, and it was certain that as soon as supplies and ammunition could be procured, an offensive operation would begin. The army and the country were electrified at this immediate effect of Grant's presence, this reversal of the entire situation; while the rebels were chagrined in an equal degree.

Still, Grant's difficulties were gigantic. Burnside's twenty-five thousand men were a hundred miles from any navigable river by which they could be supplied, and farther yet from a railroad; they had to be supplied by a route over six hundred miles long; while Sherman, in his tedious march from the Mississippi, had to be met with provisions at various points; and all these lines of supply ran through a hostile country. Grant directed and superintended these operations as closely as he did the tactical movements in a battle; he even instructed Sherman what roads he should take; he sent word to Admiral Porter to convoy the steamers that carried supplies, and that officer, never hesitating, furnished the protection desired.

But, on the 4th of November, Bragg, feeling the necessity of doing something to compensate for the disaster he had incurred at Brown's Ferry, sent an entire corps, under Longstreet, into East Tennessee, to destroy Burnside. Grant got word of the movement at once, and his situation became vastly more complicated. If Sherman had been up, he would have rejoiced at Bragg's movement, for he should at once have attacked the rebels in his front, now weakened by this abstraction. But the strength of Bragg's position, on the precipitous ridge and on the lofty crest of Lookout, was such, that no assault could be made until further reinforcements arrived. Meanwhile, Burnside was in immediate peril.

Grant at once dispatched word to Sherman of this new danger, and urged him to increased speed. Still, Sherman's difficulties were prodigious; he had rivers to cross where there were no bridges, mountains to climb, enemies to meet; but, on the 13th of November, he reached Bridgeport with his command, and was summoned at once in person to Chattanooga. In the *interim*, Grant had been urging Burnside to hold out against all odds. "I do not know how to impress on you the necessity of holding on to East Tennessee in strong enough terms." "It is of the most vital importance that East Tennessee should be held." "I can hardly conceive the necessity of retreating from East Tennessee. *If I did so at all, it would be after losing most of the army. I will not attempt to lay out a line of retreat.*" "I want the enemy's progress retarded at every point all it can be, only giving up each place when it becomes evident that it cannot longer be held without endangering your force to capture." "Can you hold the line from Knoxville to Clinton for seven days? If so, I think the whole Tennessee valley can be secured from present danger."

For Grant's strategy was here, on a larger scale, exactly what it had been at Donelson. He meant to defend Burnside by attacking Bragg. He knew well that a victorious assault on the rebel centre, would bring back this venturesome column on the rebel right. His defence was always an offence. He never was satisfied with standing still to repel attack, but wanted to make a counter attack of his own, and convert security into victory. The reasons for the extreme anxiety he felt to save East Tennessee were twofold. First, that region was filled with a loyal population, which had suffered the cruelest tortures from the rebels until a Union army had occupied the territory; and next, it was fertile beyond almost any portion of the South, and would afford immense supplies to the rebel armies if it fell once more into their hands. Besides this, it afforded a safe method of communication between Bragg and Richmond. By every moral, political, and military consideration, he was impelled, if possible, to maintain possession of East Tennessee.

But Burnside was obliged to fall back before Longstreet, although

he did not abandon Knoxville, the key-point of the country; and
Grant's anxiety became intense, lest Sherman should arrive too late.
He was once almost determined to assault before Sherman arrived, but
the lack of artillery-horses made him abandon the idea. He could
not send reinforcements to Burnside, for the enemy was directly between the two national armies; even couriers were uncertain; and
finally all communication was cut off. Still, this extraordinary man
was full of confidence. He assured the Government that Burnside
would hold out, and Sherman would arrive; that success would eventually crown his plans.

The rains, however, carried away bridges and inundated the roads,
so that it was not till the 22d of November that Grant's arrangements
were completed, and his armies in the position which he desired.

The battle-field of Chattanooga is an irregular field, with Missionary Ridge on the east and the Tennessee river on the west. On what
was Grant's left, Chickamauga creek empties into the Tennessee, and
at the extreme right is Lookout Mountain; both extremities were in
the hands of the rebels. Grant's plan was to bring Sherman along
the north side of the river, from Brown's ferry to the point opposite
Chickamauga creek, then to cross this portion of the command so as
to form his new left; Thomas was to be the centre, and to attack Missionary Ridge directly in his front; while Hooker, on the right, would
assail and carry Lookout Mountain. Sherman's principal endeavor
was to be to reach and turn the northern extremity of Missionary
Ridge, behind which was Chickamauga Station, on the southern railroad, where Bragg's base and depot of supplies were situated; Sherman was to move up from Brown's ferry along a road concealed from
the rebels by the opposite mountains; but as Bragg seemed to be expecting an attack on his left flank, Grant ordered Sherman to confirm
this notion, by advancing one division in that direction, and building
large camp-fires there at night.

At this crisis, Grant got word that Burnside and Longstreet had
really begun the battle for the possession of East Tennessee, and still
Sherman was delayed by more rains, and freshets, and broken bridges.
"I have never felt," said Grant, "such restlessness before." In consequence of these obstacles, Sherman did not arrive at his post on
the north side of the Tennessee until the 23d of November.

During the night of the 22d, however, a deserter from Bragg's army
brought news that a division of the enemy was being sent to Longstreet; and Grant had other reasons for supposing that Bragg might

be intending to fall back from Missionary Ridge. He accordingly ordered an advance by Thomas to ascertain the truth of this report. It would not do to let Bragg escape, without the battle for which the national commander had been waiting and preparing so long. Thomas accordingly moved a whole corps forward to develop the strength of the enemy. The movement was measured, and the rebels so little anticipated it, that even after the troops were in line, the rebels leaned lazily on their muskets, mistaking the advance for a parade. They were soon undeceived by a heavy fire of musketry, and in fifteen minutes their whole advanced line of rifle-pits was carried, and nothing remained in the possession of the rebels west of the rifle-pits, but the line at the foot of the ridge. Entrenchments were at once thrown up by Grant, protecting the ground thus gained, and Thomas's whole army was moved forward about a mile. Only one hundred men had been killed or wounded, but over two hundred rebels were captured. This success infused great animation into the Army of the Cumberland.

Meanwhile, Sherman was laboring up on the north bank of the Tennessee. where pontoon boats were hidden in the creeks that empty from that side of the river; and during the night of the 23d these were floated to the rebel picket-station, at the mouth of the Chickamauga. Troops were landed, the enemy's pickets seized, entrenchments thrown up, and by daylight eight thousand Union soldiers were ashore. Immediately the building of the bridge began. At twenty minutes past twelve o'clock it was complete, and at one o'clock Sherman began his march at the head of twenty thousand men for the northern end of Missionary Ridge. He began the fight by three and-a-half, pushed his troops up the hill, and before night had gained possession of an important hill, which he had supposed was the extremity of Missionary Ridge; this, however, he discovered to be separated from the ridge by a deep ravine, which would cost him dear to cross. He entrenched, however, during the night, preparing for his grand attack on the morrow.

Thomas's command this day remained in the position that had been gained the day before, waiting for the two wings of the grand army to get into position for the combined effort which Grant intended to make. Hooker, meanwhile, had moved his troops against Lookout Mountain with energy and skill; and Bragg, who had become alarmed at Thomas's dispositions of the day before, withdrew a portion of the rebel force on the mountain, to reinforce his centre and right. This rendered Hooker's task easier, and by four o'clock he had climbed the mountain, in spite of prodigious natural difficulties, carried important works at its base and on the side, and established important connection with the right of Thomas's command. Thomas also connected on his left with Sherman, so that, on the night of the 24th, Grant's line was all advanced, and in direct communication. Battles had been fought by the centre, and each wing; and each had been successful. Hooker's fight had thus far been the hardest, and late in the afternoon his progress was obscured from those in the valley by heavy clouds that settled on the mountain side, so that his troops seemed fighting in mid-air. That night the rebels evacuated the crest of the mountain, falling back on Bragg; and early in the morning the stars and stripes waved on the summit of Lookout.

Grant was busy all night, sending directions to his three armies. He directed Sherman and Hooker to advance at dawn, each attracting as much force of the enemy as possible to one extremity, and, when this was accomplished, Thomas was to attack the weakened centre. Grant himself remained on a mound near Thomas's command, from which he could watch all the evolutions in the field. He was so near to Missionary Ridge, that when day dawned, Bragg's headquarters could be plainly seen.

Sherman began his attack shortly after daylight. The ground in his front was extremely difficult, and had been strongly fortified. It was held in great force, for it was the key-point of the field. If this height was carried, the rebel army was cut off from its base, and from all communication with other portions of the rebel Confederacy. Sherman assaulted with great vigor, and gained some ground; after this he repeatedly advanced, and was more than once repelled, losing, however, none of the ground originally seized. The fight here was fierce and stubborn, and Bragg repeatedly sent large reinforcements to maintain the position. Hooker, too, descended from Lookout Mountain to move against Bragg's new left. The enemy, retreating from the mountain in the night, however, had destroyed all the bridges, so that Hooker was delayed until nearly two o'clock before he reached the ridge. Sherman, meanwhile, was bearing the brunt of the battle; and Grant finally, perceiving a large rebel column moving towards Sherman, determined that the hour had come for Thomas to advance.

Accordingly, he himself gave the order, and two whole corps moved forward in one grand line against Missionary Ridge. The sight was magnificent beyond description. Sherman fighting on the north end, not five miles away, Hooker in the plain to the south, and here, at Grant's feet, four divisions of men on the run, their bayonets glancing in the afternoon sun. The rebels at the foot of the hill were unable to resist the effect of this waving, glittering mass of steel; they flung themselves in the trenches, and the national troops passed over, sending their prisoners hurriedly to the rear, across the open plain. The order had been for the men to halt when the first line of pits was carried, and to reform before they attempted to mount the hill; but now their blood was up, and it was impossible to restrain them. A tremendous fire of artillery poured down upon them from the ridge, nearly five hundred feet high, and half way up was another line of trench, from which more deadly musketry now struck down many a gallant soldier. But the line stopped not for this; the flags went on in advance, first one ahead and then another, and at last all along the ridge Grant's colors were planted on the second rebel line. Still there was another line of works on the crest, and now the ascent became almost perpendicular. The storm of musketry and artillery became more furious, but the men lay on their faces to avoid it, working their way thus up the front of the mountain. Steadily, rapidly, on they pushed; reached the parapet, poured over in a perfect tide, and carried the crest in six different places simultaneously. So instantaneous was their success, and so little anticipated, that the rebel gunners were bayoneted at their pieces, and the rebel cannon turned upon the fugitives, enfilading the line right and left, and rendering it perfectly untenable.

The enemy was seized at once with a panic which all the exertions of Bragg and his officers could not restrain; here and there, a slight resistance was offered, but the great mass of the rebel army went tumbling in confusion down the eastern side of the ridge; the national soldiers, not even stopping to reload their pieces, but driving the enemy with stones. At this moment, Hooker appeared on the rebel left, and completed the rout; Bragg was obliged not only to give up the ground in front of Thomas and Hooker, but to withdraw his right, which still offered resistance to Sherman. Grant had ridden up at once on the ridge to direct the pursuit, and forty pieces of artillery were captured in the open field. Sheridan, then a division commander in Thomas's army, pursued for seven miles. Six thousand prisoners were taken before morning. Lookout Mountain, Missionary Ridge, and all the rifle-pits in Chattanooga valley were Grant's. The great rebel army, that had threatened him so long, was routed and in disgraceful flight, and early on the 26th, Sherman took possession of Chickamauga Station.

That day and the next the pursuit was continued, Hooker in the advance. Everywhere the road was strewn with the wrecks of the dissolving army. On the 27th, Hooker came up with Bragg's rear-guard, at a gap in the mountains, and here the enemy made his last stand. A fight of several hours occurred, but the rebels finally with-drew, leaving the place in the hands of Grant, who now directed the pursuit to be discontinued. It was necessary to send reinforcements at once to Burnside.

Grant lost in this series of battles seven hundred and fifty-seven killed, four thousand five hundred and twenty-nine wounded, and three hundred and thirty missing; the rebels, three hundred and sixty-one killed, two thousand one hundred and eighty wounded, and over *six thousand prisoners, besides forty cannon.* Their loss in killed and wounded was smaller, because they fought with every imaginable advantage of cover and position. They had forty-five thousand men engaged, and Grant had about sixty thousand; but the extraordinary position they occupied was worth to them, according to all the rules of the military art, five times an equal number of assailants. *Bragg said, in his official report of the fight, that the strength of the position was such, that a line of skirmishers ought to have maintained it against any assaulting column.*

No battle was ever fought more exactly according to the plan laid down in advance. Hooker drew attention to the right, Sherman forced the enemy to mass in his front, just as had been designed, and Thomas was made to attack the weakened centre at the critical moment, and more than the results hoped for were achieved. Armies were moved to fight this battle, from the Mississippi and the Potomac, and came up in time; mountains were climbed, rivers bridged and crossed under fire, ridges scaled, though held by hostile armies, and the enemy him-self took his part in the plan exactly as had been foreseen, as if he too had been under the orders of Grant. No prouder triumph of military skill can be achieved than this. Three separate forces con-tended on the Union side; Grant's old troops from Vicksburg did the hardest fighting under Sherman, worthy of their old renown; and, holding the great mass of the enemy at the key-point of the battle, made all the successes possible; Thomas's army, now directly under the eye of Grant, rivalled the proudest achievements that his famous veterans had ever performed; while, for the first time, soldiers from the army of the Potomac were marshalled under the orders of him with whose name that army's fame was destined to be forever and so gloriously associated.

Chattanooga secured, Chickamauga avenged, the road to Atlanta and to the sea laid bare, Tennessee protected, Georgia and Alabama threatened—these were the results of the battle fought on the 24th, 25th, and 26th of November, 1863. The battle of Chattanooga, however, did not really end until the fight at Ringgold, on the 27th of November. The same day, Grant, who had gone on with the pursuing column, sent word to Thomas, "Direct Granger to start at once, marching as rapidly as possible to the relief of Burnside;" for Grant's victory would have been dearly purchased, splendid as it was, if Burnside had been lost. Burnside was, by this time, shut up in Knoxville, where Longstreet was besieging him with a superior force. His supplies were short, and the loyal people of the country floated stores down the river into the town by night. Grant, as has been seen, had repeatedly sent him word to hold out, promising support the instant that his own still more immediate necessities would allow. The commander did not fail to keep his word. The day after the battle of Ringgold, he returned to Chattanooga, where he discovered that Granger had not yet started. He therefore ordered Sherman to move as rapidly as possible towards Knoxville, and assume command of all the forces marching towards Burnside. The distance to Knoxville is nearly a hundred miles; the roads were bad, the supplies scanty, bridges seven hundred feet in length had been destroyed and must be rebuilt; yet, on the 5th of December, Sherman was able to dispatch to Burnside, "I can bring twenty-five thousand men into Knoxville to-morrow." In the meantime, Burnside had repelled a furious attack of the rebel army, and Longstreet, hearing of Bragg's disaster at Chattanooga, and of Sherman's advance, had already abandoned the siege and retreated in the direction of Virginia. Burnside, therefore, announced that he needed only one corps of Sherman's force; and, satisfied that his own approach had served to raise the siege of Knoxville, Sherman returned to Grant.

Thus, then, after campaigns, and battles, and marches, and sieges, was Chattanooga secured forever to the nation; Knoxville, too, was relieved, not again to be endangered by rebels; and the inhabitants of East Tennessee, who had suffered so greatly for their devotion to the Union, were emancipated from the fear as well as the reality of rebel rule. The great army of Bragg, so long defiant and terrible, was separated never to be reunited, and the gateway to Georgia passed into the possession of the soldiers of the Government, who, in their turn, could assume the offensive, and threaten the interior of the States so faithful to treason. The President issued a proclamation, appointing a day of thanksgiving to God for these great benefits. Congress voted thanks to Grant and to all under his command, and a gold medal was presented to Grant in the name of the people of the United States of America. The nation knew no bounds in its gratitude to its saviour.

At this time overtures were made to Grant by prominent politicians of both parties, who solicited him to become their candidate for the Presidency. He, however, felt that his duty was to remain in the field until the rebellion should be crushed, and turned a deaf ear to the entreaties of all who approached him on this errand.

But, if he could not or would not assume the entire control of the Government, the country was determined that to him alone should be committed the entire charge of its military affairs. Nowhere, except where he had commanded, had any great success attended our arms; the gallantry of the soldiers was as conspicuous in other fields, the devotion of the country was as earnest elsewhere, the supplies as persistent, but everywhere else defeat or successful resistance had repelled our advance. Grant alone had chained victory to his standards. He alone had never been defeated. He had opened the Mississippi, the Tennessee, and the Kentucky rivers, had captured Donelson and Vicksburg, had secured Georgia, and annihilated three separate rebel armies; the nation imperatively demanded that he should be placed at the head of its soldiers.

LIEUTENANT GENERAL.

Within ten days after his victory of Chattanooga, a bill was introduced into Congress, creating a new grade in the American army, to be conferred upon Grant. The grade was that of lieutenant general; it had been borne by no American but Washington; and with it was to be conferred on the successor of Washington the command of all the armies; a command more than tenfold larger than any which the Father of his Country ever enjoyed. This bill was passed by immense majorities in both houses; and on the 1st of March, the President appointed Grant to the most important position ever filled by an American. The Presidency itself dwindled into insignificance before this office—this absolute command of half a million of soldiers, at the crisis of the nation's history. The day after the nomination was made, the Senate confirmed it, and Grant was notified on the 3d of March to report in person to the Secretary of War, at Washington. On the 4th, he started for the capital.

He had used no influence to bring about this result. One of his biographers says: "I was with him while the bill was being debated, and spoke to him more than once on the subject. He never manifested any anxiety or even desire for the success of the bill; nor did he ever seem to shrink from the responsibilities it would impose upon him. If the country chose to call him to higher spheres and more important services, whatever ability or energy he possessed, he was willing to devote to the task. If, on the contrary, he had been left at the post which he then held, he would not have felt a pang of disappointed pride." Every promotion he ever received was made without his knowledge; and even after this bill was introduced, he wrote to the introducer, saying that he had already been highly honored by the Government, and did not ask or deserve anything more in the shape of honors or promotion; that success over the enemy was what he desired above everything else. The country, however, did not put so low an estimate on his ability; it felt the need of his services in a still wider sphere, and in a more enlarged capacity than any in which they had hitherto been displayed. The country was grateful; but it was for its own sake, not his, that it now called Grant to the command of all its armies, just as it will in next November call him to the highest civil station, not in order to reward *him*, but to bring "peace, and prosperity its sequence," to our distracted land.

Before starting for Washington, Grant wrote to his true and trusted friend and coadjutor, Sherman, announcing his promotion, and with characteristic generosity and modesty attributing to Sherman, McPherson, and "many officers" who had served under him, much of the success which he had attained. "What I want is," he said, "to express my thanks to you and McPherson." "I feel all the gratitude this letter could express, giving it the most flattering construction. The word *you* I use in the plural, intending it for McPherson also." Sherman wrote in reply, "You do yourself injustice, and us too much honor, in assigning to us too large a share of the merits which have led to your high advancement." "You are now the legitimate successor of Washington, and occupy a position of almost dangerous elevation; but if you can continue, as heretofore, to be yourself—simple, honest, and unpretending—you will enjoy through

life the respect and love of friends and the homage of millions of
human beings, that will award you a large share in securing to them
and their descendants a government of law and order." The predic-
tion has been wonderfully verified. Even earlier than this, Sherman
had said, "You occupy a position of more power than Halleck or the
President. There are similar instances in European history, but none
in ours. Your reputation as a general is now far above that of any
man living. Let others manœuvre as they will, you will beat them, not
only in fame, but in doing good in the closing scenes of this war, when
somebody must heal and mend up the breaches made by war." This
almost seems prophetic, when we remember the marvellous influence
Grant possessed at the close of the war, and the wonderful use he
made of it, to secure magnanimous treatment of those whom his arms
had vanquished.

He reached Washington after a tour of four days, along the whole
route receiving one continued and enthusiastic ovation from his grateful countrymen. On his arrival at the capital, he went at once to pay
his respects to the President. He was discovered, however, at the
hotel, where he had registered his name as *U. S. Grant, Chattanooga.*
The people rose in cheers at the dining table; and, when he presented
himself. at a public levee, to the President, the throng and the enthusiasm were immense ; the President was left almost unattended, while
every one crowded around the victorious hero. On the 9th of March,
Mr. Lincoln, in the presence of his Cabinet, presented to the successor
of Washington his commission of lieutenant general, assuring him of
the nation's appreciation of what he had done, and its reliance upon
him for what remained to be done in the great struggle. " With this
high honor," he said, "devolves upon you also a corresponding responsibility; as the country herein trusts you, so, under God, it will
sustain you." A promise that the country faithfully fulfilled, and
to which it is not likely now to prove recreant. Grant replied in
simple language, befitting the dignity of the occasion, so far beyond
any eloquence but that of truth and earnestness. "I accept the commission, with gratitude for the high honor conferred. With the aid
of the noble armies that have fought in so many fields for our common
country, it will be my earnest endeavor not to disappoint your expectations. I feel the full weight of the reponsibilities now devolving
on me ; and I know that if they are met, it will be due to those armies,
and, above all, to the favor of that Providence which leads both nations
and men"—a Providence which did not desert him then, and will not

now. The aid, too, of those noble armies which he invoked, was not lacking during the war, nor will it fail him in the contest in which he is now engaged, and upon which he characteristically says he would not have entered, had he not supposed himself again to represent those whom he led in the great struggle for national existence. Providence and the mass of loyal men being again on the side of Grant, he will again trample down those same hosts in the political battle-field whom he conquered so signally in war. For it is the same men, whether at the South or at the North, who opposed him with arms or with slander, while the rebellion lasted, who now wish his downfall. It is the same men whom he will again force to unconditionally surrender.

PLAN OF CAMPAIGNS FOR 1864.

On the 17th of March, 1864, Grant assumed command of all the armies of the United States, announcing that his headquarters would be in the field, and, for the present, with the Army of the Potomac. Hitherto, during the war, the commander-in-chief of the army had remained at Washington; but Grant preferred to be present in person, where he could direct the operations of the force whose movements should seem most important. That force at present was the Army of the Potomac. At the West, the Mississippi river was free again, and the victory at Chattanooga had laid open still another path to the sea. This path Grant himself had meant to follow, and early in January had so announced to the Government, as well as to his own most important subordinates. His plan had been to fight his way to Atlanta, and thence to move either to Mobile or Savannah, as events should dictate. But he now determined to turn over this operation to Sherman, and, while he still directed that officer and all others in the army—to command in person the force whose duty was the preservation and protection of the national capital, as well as the destruction of the army that covered and defended Richmond. This rebel host had long threatened Washington; it had twice invaded the loyal States, and thus far had repelled with slaughter every attack made on it by national commanders. Until it should be annihilated, the life of the nation was not safe, no matter what victories were gained elsewhere. Its destruction had proven the most difficult task of all those intrusted to Union generals, and this, therefore, the new commander-in-chief assigned to himself. "Like yourself," said Sherman, "you take the biggest load."

6

But although present with the Army of the Potomac, Grant meant also to direct the movements of all the others. Up to this time, to use his own expressive simile, the armies, East and West, had acted like a "balky team, no two ever pulling together." The new man at the reins meant to control the team, and drive its members all in one direction. For this he needed a clear eye, a strong and skillful hand, a certainty of the goal which he meant to reach, and a fearless determination to attain that goal in spite of all or any obstacles. The rebels, so far, had acted in unison, and many a time moved troops from a less-threatened quarter to another more vigorously pressed; having the inside lines, they could do this more expeditiously, and thus often made their smaller resources in reality as available as the larger but more widely-separated armies of the nation. Grant determined to put an end to all this; no longer to allow any rest to the rebels, but to attack them everywhere, simultaneously and continuously, without regard to seasons or weather; no longer to allow the strength of the loyal troops to be neutralized by the defensive position and the superior skill of the enemy.

Accordingly, he issued orders for Sherman to move against Atlanta and Johnston, on the very day that the Army of the Potomac, under Meade, should commence operations against Lee; and, at the same time, General Butler was to attack Richmond, Sigel was to move two smaller forces into Virginia; and Banks, with all the force he could muster, was to attack Mobile, thus threatening the rear of the rebels in front of Sherman, and opening a way for that commander when he should march south to the sea. This was the original plan with which Grant set out to conquer the rebellion, after he assumed command of of the armies of the United States. This plan was entirely his own; no one suggested it; no one knew of it until it was conceived by him. Even then, not a dozen men knew it, until it had absolutely been begun. Mr. Lincoln wrote to Grant, just before the armies moved, in the following words:

"EXECUTIVE MANSION, WASHINGTON,
"*April* 30, 1864.

"Lieutenant General GRANT:

"Not expecting to see you before the spring campaign opens, I wish to express in this way my entire satisfaction with what you have done up to this time, so far as I understand it. The particulars of your plans *I neither know nor seek to know.* You are vigilant and self reliant, and pleased with this, I wish not to obtrude any restraints or constraints upon you. While I am very anxious that any great disaster or capture of our men in great numbers shall be avoided, I know that these points are less likely to escape your attention than they would be mine. If there be anything wanting which is within my power to give, do not fail to let me know it. And now, with a brave army and a just cause, may God sustain you.

" Yours, very truly,
"A. LINCOLN."

But Grant's plan met with an obstruction before it was fairly begun; an obstruction that necessitated a change, or an omission rather, at the start. General Banks, whom Grant had ordered to attack Mobile with fifty thousand men, had been sent, before Grant became lieutenant general, on an expedition west of the Mississippi, and up the Red river. As soon as Grant assumed command, he sent orders for Banks to return, abandoning this preposterous and outside enterprise, which could do nothing towards securing the main military objects of of the war, and was using up troops that might be so much better employed elsewhere. But before Grant's orders reached Banks, the latter had got so far into the interior of Louisiana, that it was impossible for him to return without fighting the enemy, stirred up now by the national advance; and the battle which ensued resulted disastrously for Banks. His army was so broken up, that it could not be counted on for effective operations in the grand combination of movements which Grant had planned. The news of this misfortune did not reach the commander-in-chief till a short time before he was ready to move his other armies; it was a great disappointment; but there was no time for other arrangements, and he determined to proceed with the rest of his plan exactly as had been proposed.

He established his headquarters at Culpeper, Virginia, in the last days of March, 1864; and from this point sent orders to all his various commanders; to Sherman, and Sigel, and Butler, and Banks, while Meade was only a few miles distant, and visited him daily. The first duty of all was concentration. No troops were to be wasted holding unimportant positions; none to be scattered over the North, except when it was indispensable. Furloughs were revoked, officers and men ordered to their posts; armies organized, supplied forwarded, and when the spring rains ceased, the various forces were ready to move.

The situation at that time was as follows: the Army of the Potomac, ninety-seven thousand strong, lay on the north bank of the Rapidan, covering Washington and opposing Lee's army, which was seventy-three thousand in number, and immediately south of the Rapidan, covering and defending Richmond. Butler had a force of nearly thirty thousand men at the mouth of the James, which he was ordered to transport suddenly up that river, landing on the south side, at City Point and Bermuda Hundred, and thence to move against Richmond, at the same time that the Army of the Potomac attacked Lee. A force nearly equal to his own opposed Butler, under Beauregard. Grant hoped either to force Lee to fall back, in order to save Richmond, or, if the main rebel army remained to fight, near the Rapidan, that Butler might slip in and capture the enemy's capital. Along the northern line of Virginia, it was necessary to maintain a Union force, in order to protect the North against invasion. These were the troops under Sigel, ten or twelve thousand strong, but instead of keeping them on the defensive, Grant determined to move them to the interior of Virginia, so as to threaten the enemy in rear, and compel him either to subtract from his main force, under Lee, in order to guard the exposed region, or to run the risk of losing that region altogether. Other commanders had been content with simply holding the line of northern Virginia, but Grant converted the troops employed for this purpose into an offensive force; not with a view of making any one prodigious and positive effort with them, but to threaten and confuse and worry and weaken the enemy. About ten thousand rebels, under Breckinridge, were in Sigel's front. Sherman, meanwhile, was at Chattanooga, with all the force that could be accumulated there, ready to move against the main rebel army of the West, now under Jos. E. Johnston. Sherman's objective point was Johnston's army; this Grant directed him to follow wherever it went, to fight it whenever he could, and to advance as far as possible into the heart of Georgia, in the direction of Atlanta, the great railroad centre of the entire southwest. When Atlanta fell, he was to push through to the sea, cutting the so-called Confederacy in two once more, as Grant had done when he opened the Mississippi river.

Grant's own objective was to be Lee's army. He was firm in the conviction that no peace could be had, that would be stable and conducive to the happiness of the people, both North and South, until the military power of the rebellion was entirely broken; and it was the military forces, rather than the fortified towns, which he made the objects of all his campaigns. Meade was instructed that wherever Lee went, he would go too. Grant meant to use the greatest number of troops practicable against the *armed force* of the enemy; this view he kept constantly in mind, and in this view all his orders were given, and all his campaigns made. When he began his operations, the rebels still held a territory over eight hundred thousand square miles in extent, and maintained a population of nine millions in revolt. All west and south of the Arkansas river was in their possession, and east of the Mississippi nearly all the region south of the Tennessee. All of Virginia south of the Rapidan, except the mouth of the James, and thence south, all the territory of the Union, except a narrow strip along the Atlantic coast, was also in the hands of the enemy. To rescue this vast region, and to overcome this population and its armies, was the herculean task undertaken by Ulysses S. Grant. No greater was ever achieved by the most renowned soldiers in history. The enemy was of the same race as his own troops; brave, experienced, numerous, desperate; acquainted with the country, of which the national forces were ignorant, skillfully led, and possessing all the immense advantages of a defensive position. But Grant did not , flinch at the prospect.

On the 4th of May, his armies were ready to move. That day Meade crossed the Rapidan with the Army of the Potomac, moving to the right and east of Lee, and placing himself so as to face west and south; the same day Sherman moved out from Chattanooga against Johnston, and Butler started for City Point, while the two forces into which Sigel's command was divided, were also simultaneously put in motion. A more striking instance of concert in movement was never known in war. Here were five different armies, numbering more than two hundred thousand men, and separated by thousands of miles, all directed by one man, and moving on the same day. That night, after Grant had crossed the Rapidan, he received dispatches by telegraph from Sherman and Butler and Sigel, announcing the operations of the day.

WILDERNESS CAMPAIGN.

Lee made no attempt to interrupt Grant's crossing, but early on the morning of the 5th of May, he came out of his entrenchments at Mine Run, a creek running north into the Rapidan, and attacked the Army of the Potomac while it was getting into position. Grant put his troops in line as quickly as possible, and the battle of the Wilderness began. It raged all day with unequal success, and at night neither party could claim a victory. The forest was dense and the roads narrow, and it was difficult to manœuvre troops; indeed, no artillery at all could be used. On the 6th, the battle was renewed with unabated fury, and one of the most remarkable conflicts of the war ensued. There was no cessation until night, and even after dark an attempt was made to turn Grant's right, but failed. No decided success had been achieved by either party, and on the 7th neither seemed inclined to renew the fight. Lee's effort to force Grant back across the Rapidan, as Hooker and Burnside and Meade had successively been forced before, had failed; but Grant had not been able to drive Lee from the position first assumed; and there the great armies lay, like two wild beasts exhausted after the terrible struggle, glaring at each other, neither mortally wounded, each ready to spring to the defence if the other should assail.

As it was apparent that Lee did not mean to assume the offensive again, Grant at once issued orders for a movement to the left towards Spottsylvania Court House, which would probably force Lee in the same direction, for otherwise Grant could place his whole army between the rebels and Richmond. Few other generals would have dreamed of taking this responsibility, of advancing after so terrible a battle in which no decisive advantage had been gained; and leaving Lee, if he chose, to move upon Grant's rear, or even in the direction of Washington. But to return, or even to be stayed in his course, did not occur to Grant. He would have asked nothing better than that Lee should move North, presenting his own flank to Grant in the act; but he was confident that too much injury had been sustained by his rebel antagonist to leave him able or willing to undertake this. With all the grimness and determination with which he had maintained his own at Shiloh; in the same spirit in which he had persevered at Vicksburg; with a daring equal to that displayed at Donelson, when in the blackest moment he ordered another charge, Grant now turned the head of his column towards Richmond, while Lee still lay formidable in his front. He thus not only made one of the most hazardous of military operations, a flank movement in the presence of the enemy; but, what was of far more moment, he displayed to his own army and to Lee's the peculiar character of his nature, which difficulties never deter nor dangers appall; his conduct impressed the rebels so that they did not attempt to interrupt his movement despite the opportunity, and it

inspired his own soldiers with the temper of their commander. When
he rode along their ranks at night, with his horse's head towards Richmond, all stiff with fatigue and sore with wounds as they were, they
rose from their beds on the battle-field, amid the corpses of their
slaughtered comrades, and shouted for the chief who proved to them
that the slaughter and the toil were not to be in vain. It was a pledge
to the army that they should not turn their faces away from Richmond
until it was taken; the army accepted the pledge, and their huzzas
were the endorsement they gave to their new commander. They
cheered, indeed, so loud, that the enemy thought there was another
assault, and came out to meet it. And thus Grant passed on after
the great battle of the Wilderness, tacitly promising his soldiers that
reward, which they were a year, it is true, in gaining, but which finally
came, more complete and glorious than the most sanguine had ever
dared to anticipate. This midnight ride was the fitting precursor of
Appomattox Court House. Four days after, Grant sent his famous
dispatch: "*I propose to fight it out on this line if it takes all summer.*"
It did take all summer, and all winter too, but Grant remained on the
same line, and, when that was fought out, the rebellion was ended.

The enemy, however, at once discovered the movement, and, falling
rapidly back, as Grant had supposed, reached Spottsylvania before
him, which was not what he desired. But the line from Lee's army to
Spottsylvania was shorter than Grant's route by some miles. The
marching was done in the night of the 7th, and on the 8th an attack
was made by Grant at Spottsylvania. It did not succeed. On the
9th, 10th, and 11th, the Union army was constantly engaged in
manœuvring and fighting, but without result. On the 12th, a vigorous
attack was made on the rebel line, now defended by field works of
unusual strength, and at one place the 2d corps, under Hancock,
succeeded in carrying an important salient, capturing an entire division of rebel infantry and twenty pieces of artillery; the subsequent
resistance, however, was so obstinate, that even this success did not
prove decisive. The loss of life on both sides had now been large,
and Grant sent back to Washington for reinforcements, while Lee did
the same to Richmond. A week was spent in manœuvring and waiting for these fresh troops. The rebels, however, made no assault in
all this time, on Grant, contenting themselves with the defensive. On
the 19th of May, however, a rebel corps came out of its works on the
extreme right of Grant, and attacked him with great fury, but was
repulsed with immense loss. This was the last attack in force ever

made by Lee on Grant, though the war lasted ten months longer. The battles of the Wilderness and of Spottsylvania so crippled the rebel strength and affected the rebel spirits, that their commander never again dared trust his troops outside of their works in any great assault. Grant now determined to renew the tactics to which he had resorted after the Wilderness; and, on the night of the 21st, he began another movement by the left flank, towards the North Anna river, with a view again of placing himself between Lee and Richmond. Of course, he exposed himself to the same risk of Lee getting between him and Washington, but he always took risks; and Lee never ventured to avail himself of the chance. As fast as Grant threatened to cut off the rebel communications, the enemy fell back to protect them, and thus, when Grant reached the North Anna, Lee was there before him, having necessarily, from his position in all these movements, the shorter line. The North Anna, however, was crossed by a portion of Grant's army, despite severe opposition.

Meanwhile, Butler had moved promptly, on the 4th of May, siezed City Point, at the mouth of the Appomattox river, as well as Bermuda Hundred, on the opposite bank of that stream. His movements for some days afterwards, however, were not productive of any result of importance. On the 13th and 14th, he moved up to the rear of Drury's Bluff, a fort on the south side of the James, and about seven miles below Richmond. But the rebels had meantime collected all their scattered forces in North and South Carolina; and, on the 16th, they attacked Butler, and forced him back to his entrenchments between the forks of the James and Appomattox, where he was completely safe indeed, but entirely useless for offensive operations. Lee, in consequence, was able to reinforce his army in front of Grant with at least a division brought from before Richmond. Sigel's operations had also been unfortunate; he had advanced up the Valley of Virginia, as far as New Market, where he suffered a severe defeat, and retreated behind Cedar creek. In consequence of this result, Lee was able to bring several thousand reinforcements from the Valley of Virginia to oppose the Army of the Potomac.

Grant, however, learning that rebel troops had been moved from Butler's front to reinforce Lee, immediately ordered Butler to send all his available force to the Army of the Potomac, retaining only enough on the south side of the James to secure what had already been gained.

Before these reinforcements reached Grant, he had made a third movement to the left, finding that the position of the rebels on the North Anna was stronger than either of those they had previously held. On the night of the 26th, the Union forces withdrew to the north bank of the North Anna, then marched south and east, and crossed the Pamunkey river at Hanovertown. The enemy, however, made a corresponding movement, and, when Grant arrived at Cold Harbor, and the Chickahominy, Lee was again in his front.

The additions to the forces on each side had brought the armies of both Lee and Grant up to nearly the numbers with which they started from the Rapidan, when both approached Cold Harbor, about ten miles from Richmond. Several indecisive conflicts occurred here, and, on the 3d of June, Grant ordered a general assault upon the enemy's works, but met with the same result as at Spottsylvania; the enemy, behind his bulwarks, was doubled in strength, according to all the estimates of the military art, and the national troops were unsuccessful in the attempt to penetrate the works. This was the only encounter of the campaign in which Grant did not inflict upon the enemy a damage which compensated for his own. All the other battles had resulted in what he had been striving to accomplish—in such a terrible weakening of the enemy, that his own losses were endurable for the sake of inflicting on the rebels what they were so much less able to sustain. Every battle fought thus far had tended plainly to the complete overthrow of the rebellion. And this was what Grant set out to accomplish. It was what none of his predecessors had succeeded in doing, in three years of effort, and loss, and failure. It had been sadly proven in those three years that only through great loss and effort could that result be attained; and, when he started from the Rapidan, Grant made up his mind that only the annihilation of Lee's army, and the exhaustion of all the rebel forces, would allow the suppression of the rebellion. All these battles—of the Wilderness, of Spottsylvania, and Cold Harbor—were fought and persisted in with the intention of gradually weakening and finally destroying Lee. They effected their purpose, at the price of precious lives, it is true, but at that price the Union was saved, and could alone be saved; all other means had failed; no skill had proved sufficient, no courage had availed, until Grant came, and dealt those tremendous blows, which were the real death blows from which the rebellion never recovered. They did what he set out to do.

They not only depleted Lee so terribly that he never again assaulted Grant, but they drove the rebel commander step by step from the Rapidan to the James, from which he never afterwards advanced except in the direction of Appomattox Court House. Grant at Cold Harbor was master of the region between Richmond and Washington; his communication with the latter city was open, while the rebels were shut up within the doomed town, which so many of our leaders had striven to reach in vain.

When Grant started from the Rapidan, it had been his intention to cross the James and attack Richmond on the south side, unless he should sooner overthrow Lee on the way. The situation of Richmond is peculiar; it is supplied from the south by three railroads, that run, one, the Weldon road, directly into North Carolina, and so on through the Atlantic States; another, reaching west to Chattanooga, and connecting with the entire southwestern region of the attempted Confederacy; the third, running southwest into the interior, as far as Danville. Grant saw, by a glance at the map, that when these railroads were in his power, Richmond must fall. Before the campaign began, he declared to those in his confidence, his intention to seize these roads, as soon as Lee should be driven into Richmond. This was now accomplished. Lee was within ten miles of the city which he defended and Grant besieged. Lee's army and Richmond were now become one objective point, and Grant at once set about carrying out the secondary plan he had formed six weeks before.

He marched his army across the James, making a fourth movement to the left, in the very sight of the enemy, who was too weak and had suffered too greatly to come out and obstruct the operation. Grant's pickets were within hailing distance of Lee's; his army front was not five hundred yards from the rebel works at Cold Harbor; but he withdrew his forces from this close propinquity, made a fourth flank movement in the very presence of his enemy, built bridges across the James two thousand two hundred feet in length, and crossed his whole army, with an immense wagon train, without the loss of a man, Lee not daring to come out of his works once, not offering the slightest opposition to an operation of such combined delicacy and magnitude. No better proof of the damage the rebel commander had sustained could be offered or required.

During this campaign, Grant had fought the battles of the Wilderness, Spottsylvania, North Anna, and Cold Harbor, besides a dozen smaller skirmishes, some of which rose to the proportions of an ordinary battle; and after each fight, he had advanced and Lee had withdrawn. While covering and protecting Washington, the Union commander had steadily proceeded from the Rapidan to the James. He had lost, from the 5th of May to the 12th of June, six thousand killed, twenty-six thousand wounded, and nearly seven thousand missing; total, less than forty thousand men, of whom half eventually returned to duty. The losses of the rebels can never be definitely known, as so many of their records have been destroyed; but Grant captured in this period over ten thousand of the enemy, while his own loss in missing, as has already been stated, was less than seven thousand; doubtless, most of these were prisoners; so that Grant took about four thousand more prisoners than Lee. It is fair to suppose, then, that Lee's other losses (in killed and wounded) at least equalled those of Grant.

In comparing the losses in this campaign with those of Grant's predecessors, it should not be forgotten, that Grant was victorious, and the other repelled; yet Grant's entire loss was forty thousand. In the great European battles, the losses were very much greater. At Jena, twenty thousand Prussians and fourteen thousand French were put *hors du combat* on one day; at Eylau, the losses were twenty-five thousand on one side, and thirty thousand on the other; at Wagram, twenty-five thousand on a side; at Borodina, fifty thousand on a side; at Leipsic, sixty thousand on one side, and forty-three thousand on the other; and at Waterloo, the French lost forty thousand, and the allies forty-nine thousand; so that frequently, in a single battle, as many men were killed or wounded as Grant lost in the whole Wilderness campaign.

CO-OPERATIVE CAMPAIGNS OF GRANT.

Grant's army was now thrown rapidly on the southern side, he still *fighting it out on the original line;* for, as has been seen, all this was in consummation of the plan he had announced to his subordinates before he left the Rapidan. He was still following Lee and aiming at Richmond. The James river was crossed on the 13th of June, 1864.

Meanwhile, Hunter, who had superseded Sigel, was sent into the region to the northwest of Richmond, with the idea of living off the country there, so as to destroy its supplies, and, if possible, cut the rebel communication with the West. By this expedition, and another simultaneously dispatched under Sheridan towards Staunton, Virginia, Grant meant to act upon the principle with which he set out, of weakening the enemy in every quarter at once. While he himself should

be making the main attack at the heart of the rebellion, his subordinates, in every part of the theatre of war, were to exhaust, and
annoy, and tire out the rebels, to prevent them from concentrating,
or recruiting, or reinforcing, or resting, so that when the final blow
should be given at the vital part, that should indeed be the end.

In this way all the campaigns were made coöperative; all were subordinate to his own, the most difficult of all. Sherman and Hunter
and Butler had all been assisting him to carry out that unity in the
movements which he had conceived, for all the while he was fighting
Lee he was directing all his subordinates. Every day he got dispatches from Sherman and sent him orders in reply. That great soldier was accustomed to report his situation daily to his chief, and ask,
"Shall I fight to-day or to-morrow? do you want me to move to the
right or to the left?" He knew the absolute necessity of his doing
everything so as to contribute to carry out Grant's scheme; he felt
that he was not fighting an independent campaign; that he was but part
of a great whole, which Grant was managing and controlling; and
with grand and patriotic subordination, he was content with his part,
and never interfered with Grant's views, or sought to set up for himself what might perhaps have been better for his own army, but worse,
in the end, for the great result at which the chief was aiming.

This should be constantly kept in mind, in studying these campaigns.
The movements in Virginia were strictly coöperative. They, too,
were only a part; their aim and object are obscured, their greatness
is not sufficiently apparent, if it is forgotten that Grant was at the
same time directing operations all over the continent; that he thought
it worth while to incur great risk here, because he thus withheld the
rebels from reinforcing their armies a thousand miles away. For
Sherman was by this means able to slowly penetrate into Georgia.
By the time Grant had crossed the James, Sherman had driven Johnston back in battle and on the march as far as Kenesaw mountain, a
distance of fifty miles, and Hunter had reached and invested Lynchburg. So all the strings pulled by the master-hand were at work;
the complicated movements of the vast machine all went slowly but
surely on. Some delay here and there occurred; great difficulties often
stood in the way; but the work proceeded. At the end of what is
called the Wilderness Campaign, Grant had reached the James river;
the other great armies of the Republic were also penetrating to the
very interior of the rebel region; the practical concentration that had
been aimed at was being effected; the rebels were losing heart and

men and resources, as well as ground, all of which could never be regained; and though the price that had been paid was great, not otherwise or cheaper could the result have been obtained. Through fire and blood and suffering only are nations saved. Grant had every reason to be satisfied that his plans had proceeded thus far to their consummation. The enemy felt certainly that the toils were being drawn closer on every side; that their new antagonist was a master; that unity of action and clearness of design and energy of effort had succeeded to distraction, and indecision, and spasmodic struggles on the part of the Union. So far, the nation had great cause for gratitude to God and its armies, and to him who, under God, was the leader of those armies.

Before Grant began to remove the Army of the Potomac to the southern side of the James, he dispatched Sheridan, as has been seen, upon another of those raiding expeditions which formed so important a part of his plan. It was his constant aim to destroy the communications of the enemy, and this was especially necessary to be done on the north side of Richmond, at the moment when Grant was planning to remove his own army to the southern side. He wanted to make it impossible for Lee either to draw any supplies of consequence from the region north of the James, or to have such use of the railroads running towards Washington as would enable him to threaten the national capital. Sheridan, therefore, had been sent to destroy the Virginia Central railroad, at the same time that Hunter had been moved south from Winchester, on the route that Sigel had attempted at the outset of the campaign. The region where Hunter was to operate is known as the Valley of Virginia, and is one of the most fertile spots in the Union. It had furnished supplies of vast importance to the rebels all through the war, and was the only really important source yet left open to Lee on the north side of Richmond. Grant planned for Sheridan and Hunter to advance towards each other, from opposite directions, doing all the destruction possible to railroads, canals, and crops, and forming a junction in the heart of the fruitful region. After the work laid out for them was thoroughly done, they were to join the Army of the Potomac; either making a circuit in the rear of Lee, or returning by Sheridan's route, as should seem most advisable at the time.

It should be constantly borne in mind, that all these raiding movements were ventures, and looked upon as such by Grant. They were attempts, at great risk, to accomplish certain objects: the destruction of certain stores, or resources, or communications; if that destruction was consummated, even at the sacrifice of the command which accomplished it, the raid was a success. It was often worth while to pay the price of the utter capture of a small command for the sake of securing some definite object; just as, in the capture of a town by assault, the forlorn hope which attacks is almost certain to be lost; but it is better and more humane to lose a small command in a single assault, than to waste away a large one in a protracted siege or a series of ineffective movements. The difference is, that in these raids, the command, if lost, was probably only captured, not killed.

These remarks have no peculiar application to the movement of Hunter or Sheridan; neither force was captured or annihilated; each accomplished the particular duty for which it was dispatched. Hunter drove the enemy in his front, occupied temporarily nearly all the Valley of Virginia, fought a battle in which he carried everything before him, while Sheridan moved up in the same direction, though from a different starting-point, doing great damage to railroads and crops. But Hunter thought it advisable to move westward instead of towards Sheridan, as had been planned and ordered; so the junction was not formed, and Sheridan, meeting with greater opposition than his force alone was able to overcome, returned to Grant, while Hunter marched direct on Lynchburg, a place of the greatest importance in the rear of Richmond. Lee at once perceived the necessity of retaining Lynchburg, and dispatched a large force, under Early, to oppose Hunter. Grant had not hoped that Hunter, without Sheridan, would be able to capture Lynchburg, which, being on the Chattanooga railroad, must of necessity be vigorously defended by Lee; but Hunter had been so successful thus far, that he made the attempt. Lee, however, having, as usual, a greatly shorter line, threw a force into Lynchburg before Hunter reached it; and Hunter, getting short of ammunition, was obliged to retire. He had now no choice of routes, but was obliged to return north by way of the Kanawha valley; and this occupied him several weeks, during which the region that it was intended he should cover was necessarily left exposed

PETERSBURG

Unfortunately, all this happened at the very moment when Grant was making his movement across the James. Grant, not knowing of Hunter's change of plan, supposed of course that the latter was protecting the Shenandoah valley; and proceeded with his movement to the south side. W. F. Smith, who was in command of the troops from Butler's army, was moved out in the night to White House, on the York river, where he took transports, which conveyed him by the Chesapeake bay and James river, to City Point and Bermuda Hundred. Butler, thus reinforced with his own troops, was to seize Petersburg, a point in the interior lying directly on the road to Richmond. It was impossible to advance farther up the James river than Bermuda Hundred, on account of the elaborate defences with which that stream was guarded. Grant, however, hoped to secure Petersburg by surprise, before the enemy could become aware of his intention or fortify the place. Smith moved with great secrecy and celerity, and meanwhile Grant had directed the laying of a pontoon-bridge over the James, by which the Army of the Potomac was to cross. The bridge was laid some twenty miles from Petersburg, which is on the Appomattox, about ten miles in a direct line from the James. The idea was for Smith, who went on transports, to advance rapidly and seize Petersburg, while the Army of the Potomac would cross by the bridge and march up at once to his support. Smith reached Petersburg early on the 15th of June, but did not assault until sundown; he then attacked with a part of his force, and carried a portion of the rebel lines with ease, capturing fifteen cannon and three hundred prisoners by seven o'clock p. m. Meanwhile, the advance of the Army of the Potomac had been hurried across the James, extraordinary exertions had been made to supply it with rations, and it was pushed rapidly forward to the support of Smith. Hancock was in command of this advance. He reached Petersburg before dark, and, being the senior officer, was entitled to command. As Smith, however, had already gained so great advantages, Hancock waived his rank and offered his troops to Smith, to be used as that officer should desire. Smith, however, thought he had accomplished enough, and although it was a bright moonlight night, and there were no indications that the rebels were reinforced, he did not push the assault. In the night the enemy discovered Grant's withdrawal from the north side and the attack on Petersburg, and before morning Lee was in force in front of Hancock and Smith. Again he had the shorter line.

Grant, meanwhile, had been superintending and expediting the crossing of the Army of the Potomac, and, early on the 16th, rode up to Smith's lines, hoping to find him in possession of Petersburg; for there had been ample time, opportunity, and force. But he found the enemy fortifying, Smith occupying an outer line, with Lee in strength behind the rebel works, and it was not till evening that the Army of the Potomac was up in sufficient force to assault the now increased strength of the enemy. Attacks were made on the 16th, 17th, and 18th, and important positions gained; but the enemy could not be dislodged from his interior line. It was the old story over: Lee had the advantage of the defence, he threw up his breastworks, and it required twice as many men as Grant had to carry them.

Disappointed (through the inefficiency of Smith) in his hopes of seizing the town, Grant now determined to envelope Petersburg, not attacking fortifications again, but extending his line as far as possible towards two of the railroads, so important to Richmond, and which both passed through Petersburg. Lee, of course, perceived this change in Grant's tactics, and, as Hunter was at this time advancing against Lynchburg, the rebels were able to send off a corps with safety to repel Hunter. This accordingly was done.

But Grant was not idle, although he had determined to cease assaulting Petersburg. His aim was to reach the South-Side road, and he dispatched two small divisions of cavalry, under Wilson, to strike that road at a distance of fifteen miles from Petersburg. Wilson reached the road, and destroyed it for a distance of many miles, doing serious damage to the enemy's communications; but, in his return, he was intercepted by a force sent out by Lee to pursue him. He divided his command and endeavored to avoid the enemy, but was foiled in the attempt, and only succeeded in rejoining the Army of the Potomac with the loss of all his guns and trains. This expedition, however, illustrates the remark made above in relation to raids. Though the command suffered more than any similar expedition during the war, the damage it inflicted on the enemy fully compensated for the loss sustained.

Meanwhile, Grant had effected a lodgement on the north side of the James, at a point called Deep Bottom, some miles nearer to Richmond than City Point; and, on the 26th of July, he moved a large force to that place, crossing the James by a pontoon-bridge above Bermuda Hundred. The object of this move was, if possible, to cut again the enemy's railroads on the north side; or, if it should seem more desirable, to take advantage of the withdrawal of the enemy's troops from before Petersburg, which this demonstration on the north side would necessitate, and explode a mine which had been dug under the rebel lines at Petersburg. The enemy moved in so large force to oppose the operation from Deep Bottom, that Grant at once determined to explode the mine, and assault the works at Petersburg. He moved back a corps of troops from the north to the south side in the night, and, on the morning of the 30th of July, the mine was sprung, creating great consternation in the rebel ranks, and forming a gaping crater in the midst of their fortifications. Arrangements had been made, and orders issued, for the troops to rush in at once after the explosion, and this was promptly done; but those who were to push on in support were so long in getting to the place of action, that the enemy rallied from his surprise, and brought up forces to the defence. As the captured line was thus rendered untenable, and of itself was of no advantage, Grant withdrew his troops. The assault had been skillfully planned, the strategy which drew Lee to the north side of the · James was a master-piece of military genius, but the inefficiency of one of the subordinates converted what should have been absolute success into defeat. There was no good reason why Petersburg should not have been carried on this day.

EARLY.

Lee was an astute soldier, and as soon as he discovered that Hunter was retreating westward from Lynchburg, and that, in consequence, the Shenandoah valley was left open and Washington uncovered, he determined to avail himself of this opportunity. This opportunity was in nowise created by Grant. All of that officer's plans and orders contemplated the complete protection of Washington. The overland route from the Rapidan had been selected by him in great part with a view to affording this protection, and the campaign of Sigel was planned especially for this purpose, and to close the avenue which the Shenandoah valley would otherwise offer. The movements of the Wilderness campaign, the constant retreat of Lee, and the advance of Grant after every battle, effected this object; and, up to the moment when Grant crossed the James, there had been no occasion for apprehension in regard to the national capital. Nor was the movement to the south side, as planned by Grant, at all in contravention of his original purpose. Hunter's movement up the Shenandoah, and Sheridan's coöperative march towards Charlottesville, where the junction was to be effected, were ordered with the express view of destroying the communications north of Richmond, and making it impossible for Lee to throw any large force in the direction of the Potomac. But Hunter moved

7

on Lexington instead of towards Charlottesville, and Sheridan's force
was too small to be risked there alone; so Sheridan, after doing a
good work of destruction; returned to Grant, while Hunter, being
repelled from Lynchburg, and compelled to fall back westward instead
of to the north, left the route to Washington by the valley entirely
open to Lee.   Hunter, it is true, had accomplished much in the valley
before he quitted it; but, upon his leaving it, the highway was clear.
Lee was too wary not to perceive and avail himself of the chance.

Thus, before Grant could learn the fate of Hunter, the rebel chief
dispatched the corps which had been sent to the defence of Lynchburg
into the Shenandoah valley.   The command, now increased, was under
Early, and moved rapidly down the valley, reaching the neighborhood
of Maryland by the 1st of July.   Great alarm was immediately felt
at the national capital.   The Government had relied so exclusively on
Grant, that, he being absent in front of Petersburg, all its action
seemed paralyzed.   He was urged in the most vehement manner to
move his army at once from the James back to the Potomac, and
abandon all the advantages he had gained through the two months of
fighting and marching, in order to save the capital.   He, however,
had no idea of doing this.   He felt that he had his hand at the throat
of the rebellion, and he meant never to let go his grasp.   He saw
how vastly more important it was for him to maintain his army at the
vital military point; and he had the genius to perceive that point, as
well as the courage to do as he thought right, in spite of entreaties
and advice from soldiers and civilians of place and reputation at the
rear.

But he still had no notion of losing Washington.   He dispatched,
first one division, and then two more, of the Sixth corps, to the defence
of the region near the Potomac; he sent orders to the officials at
Washington to gather up all the forces in that neighborhood, at Baltimore, and in the garrison of the capital; and at last sent the Nineteenth
corps, which he had ordered from Banks, when he became convinced
that nothing effective against Mobile could be done with the command
of that officer during this campaign.   This corps, arriving North at
this crisis, to join the forces on the James, was immediately ordered
by Grant to Washington; so that, before the rebel force had reached
that city, the Union strength was sufficient to defend it.   Reinforcements came in rapidly from these various quarters, and Grant
telegraphed for General Wright, who commanded the Sixth corps, to be
placed at the head of all the troops for the defence of Washington;

and directed that officer to move at once on the offensive against Early. Wright obeyed promptly, and Early was driven back into the valley. Hunter now arrived, after his circuitous return from West Virginia, and joined Wright at the entrance of the valley; he was the ranking officer and took command.

Thus Lee's plan of forcing Grant to abandon Richmond, for the sake of saving Washington, was entirely defeated. It had been a skillful move on the military chessboard, and, with many other generals to deal with, would have succeeded; but Grant never wavered for a moment. He had no more idea of abandoning the goal at which he was aiming, on account of any such distraction as Early's campaign, than he had of returning to Washington after the battle of the Wilderness. He knew what was his real object, and he suffered nothing to divert his attention. Still, he was able to carry on a manifold campaign. Because he chose to direct his principal strength against a certain point, was no reason why he should not control all the subordinate movements, which were to tend to the same object, through different channels. He could drive four-in-hand, even when the team was "balky."

SHERIDAN

It was plain, however, at this time, that the rebels meant to continue to threaten Washington. They had temporarily annoyed Grant by this valley movement, and they were determined to persist in it; as, in in consequence of the addition to their strength, which the fortifications of Petersburg afforded, they were able to afford the subtraction of enough men to create a serious distracting element in Grant's campaign near home. This seemed like good policy, and would have been good, had not Grant been Grant. As it was, Lee annoyed his antagonist considerably for a while, until the Union commander became provoked, and finally turned and dealt a blow to the rebels from which they never recovered. The weapon with which he dealt the blow was Sheridan.

The confusion, and mismanagement, and alarm around Washington, during all these movements, had convinced Grant that there existed the same necessity for one supreme commander of all the forces in the neighborhood of the capital, which had been felt for a chief of all the armies, until he himself became lieutenant general. He determined that the four departments of West Virginia, Washington, Susquehannah, and the Middle Department must be consolidated, and that a capable soldier must be placed at the head of them, who could be allowed sufficient independence of action and discretion to secure success in his movements, but who at the same time must be really subordinate, and willing to make the movements of his command thoroughly coöperative with those more important ones of the army in front of Lee. Grant, therefore, visited Washington in person, informed the Government of his views, to which they immediately deferred, and then went forward to the valley to view the situation for himself, and determined what he wanted done, and by whom. He at once decided that the true course was to concentrate all the troops in that region, and push the enemy as far as possible. He, indeed, never believed in remaining on the defensive. Sheridan, as commander of the cavalry of the Army of the Potomac, had already displayed the characteristics, the splendid vigor, the persistency, the determination, the sagacity, and the moral courage which Grant required for the position he was now creating. He sent for Sheridan, who joined him at Monocacy, Maryland, and then placed in command the illustrious soldier who was destined to achieve immortality for himself in this new field, while adding to the laurels already so thick on the brows of Grant. Sheridan was directed, "Concentrate all your available force; and if it is found that the enemy has moved north of the Potomac in large force, push North, follow him, attack him, wherever he can be found. Follow him, if driven south of the Potomac, as long as it is safe to do so." Two divisions of his old cavalry were sent from the Army of the Potomac, to assist in carrying out these orders; and he was informed, "In pushing up the Shenandoah valley, it is desirable that nothing should be left to invite the enemy to return. Take all provisions, forage, stock, wanted for the use of your command; such as cannot be consumed, destroy. The people should be informed that so long as an army can subsist among them, recurrences of these raids must be expected, and we are determined to stop them at all hazards. Bear in mind the object is to drive the enemy south, and to do this *you want to keep him always in sight.* Be guided in your course by the course he takes."

These orders contain a synopsis of Grant's entire military policy. They show that he believed in always taking the offensive, in concentration of troops and efforts, in "pushing," driving, following, attacking the enemy whenever he could be found, in *keeping him always in sight;* but that he was guided in his course by the course of the enemy—rare sagacity in a general; and that when it became necessary, he could be stern; that he knew modern war depends as much on the ability to supply armies as on the skill to wield them, and, in consequence, he always made war on the resources as well as on the troops of his enemy.

Having established Sheridan in command, and given him his orders, the lieutenant general returned to City Point, to hurry up the cavalry which was to join the new commander. It was more than a month before Sheridan could get his army ready to move, and the country, not knowing the man as Grant did, got anxious. Pennsylvania and Maryland seemed constantly threatened with invasion, and Grant paid Sheridan another visit, not being willing to give him a positive order to attack, until he should once more see for himself the exact situation. This Sheridan explained, announced he could move the moment he was ordered, and expressed every confidence of success. Grant declares that he saw there were but two words of instruction to give his subordinate—" Go in ;" *in* being, in military parlance, a condensed form for "into battle." Grant asked Sheridan if he could be ready by Tuesday, and the latter replied, " Before daylight on Monday." He did promptly what he promised, and Grant declared, " The result was such that I have never since deemed it necessary to visit General Sheridan before giving him orders."

On the 19th of September, Sheridan attacked Early and defeated him with heavy loss, capturing several thousand prisoners. The enemy rallied at Fisher's Hill, and was attacked again, and again defeated on the 20th; Sheridan pursued him with great energy. On the 9th of October, still another battle occurred at Strasburg, when the rebels were a third time defeated, losing eleven pieces of artillery. On the night of the 18th, however, they returned and attacked Sheridan's command, from which he was about twenty miles distant at the time; the national forces were driven back with loss, but finally rallied ; just at this moment Sheridan came upon the field, arranged his lines to receive a new attack of the enemy, and in his turn assumed the offensive, defeating the rebels with great slaughter, and the loss of their artillery, as well as all the trophies which had been captured in the morning. Pursuit was made to the head of the valley, and thus ended the last attempt of the rebels to invade the North. Their force in the valley was completely broken up, and never again assumed an organized independent form. Grant was thus able to bring back the Sixth corps to the Army of the Potomac, to send one division from Sheridan to the Army of the James, and another to Sherman.

On the 13th of August, Grant, fearing that Lee, in order to support Early, might be detaching from the army defending Petersburg,
moved a large force to the north side of the James, so as to threaten
Richmond from that quarter, and compel Lee to bring back any troops
he might be sending to the valley. It was discovered that only a
single division had been sent to Early; but this movement had the
effect of drawing a large rebel force from the defences of Petersburg,
in order to resist the apprehended attack on Richmond. Grant at
once determined to avail himself of this weakening of the rebel lines
before Petersburg, and sent the Fifth corps to seize the Weldon railroad, which, as yet, the rebels held, and by which they drew many of
their most important supplies. A fierce battle ensued, with heavy
losses on each side, but Grant gained possession of the road, and the
most furious efforts of the enemy were insufficient to dislodge him. He
never afterwards lost his hold of that important avenue of communication between the rebel capital and the region farther South. On
the contrary, he constructed a railroad from City Point to the Weldon
road, and was thus able to transport his own supplies to the extreme
left of his now extended front.

Miles upon miles of fortifications now defended both Richmond and
Petersburg, and the besiegers themselves had erected works as strong
as those which they opposed. The extension of Grant beyond the
Weldon road forced Lee also to reach out by his own right, or Grant
would have overlapped him. This extension of Lee, it seemed, must
weaken his force on the north side of the James; so Grant, on the
29th of September, made an advance against the fortifications of Richmond. The strongest of all the defences of that city was carried by
assault, but this was only one fort among many, and no other success
was attained. The position was, however, so important and so far
advanced, that Grant determined to maintain it. Butler's entire army
was now moved to the north of the James, to remain there. Desperate
attempts were made by the rebels to dislodge him, but all failed.
Simultaneously with the capture of this position, afterwards known as
Fort Harrison, Meade made a movement on the extreme left of the
lines before Petersburg, with a view of attacking, if the enemy should
be found materially weakened by a withdrawal of troops to Butler's

front. Several fights occurred, but no result of significance, and Meade returned.

On the 27th of October, another movement was made to the left, with the view of ascertaining whether it would be possible to overlap the enemy's right, and thus to reach the South-Side road, whose possession would at once secure the fall of Petersburg. This reconnoissance, however, developed the fact, that the enemy's fortifications reached out certainly to within six miles of the South-Side road, if not farther, and, no opening for a successful assault presenting itself, Grant returned within his own lines. In making the return movement, Hancock was attacked, but immediately faced his corps about and drove the enemy, with slaughter, within their works.

CO-OPERATION OF SHERMAN.

Meanwhile, another portion of Grant's great scheme was proceeding under the skillful management of Sherman. That commander was able to prosecute his campaign without fear of interruption. He was certain that Grant would not intermit his operations, and that no support from Lee would be allowed to come to Johnston at a critical moment. He himself was coöperating constantly with Grant, preventing Johnston from reinforcing Lee, and he had no fear that his commander would forget or neglect him. There was perfect harmony between the chief and his great lieutenant. So Sherman, moving from Chattanooga, on the 6th of May, had advanced in a series of skillful movements, somewhat similar to those of Grant in the Wilderness. The battles were not so fierce, the opposition not so obstinate, but the campaign reflected immense credit on Sherman and his army; and on the 2d of September it was crowned with success. Atlanta, the first objective designated to Sherman by Grant, was captured, the result of the last of a series of flank movements, which will always be memorable in military history. Johnston had at first been Sherman's antagonist, but falling into disfavor with the rebel authorities at Richmond, he had, in July, been superseded by Hood, an officer of vastly less ability, but with a more reckless audacity. Hood assisted Sherman materially by the unskillful character of his operations.

That which afforded not only Sherman, but Thomas and even Grant, opportunity for the conception and execution of some of their finest designs, was a movement undertaken soon after the fall of Atlanta. Of this movement, however, it is believed that Jefferson Davis is entitled to some of the credit. Sherman, having driven Hood's army

steadily back a hundred and fifty miles, and manœuvred it out of
Atlanta, the great railroad centre in Middle Georgia, Hood now
thought that, depleted and disheartened as his soldiers were, he could
assume the offensive against the force by which he had been so often
defeated. Making a wide detour, he advanced to the right of Sherman, and moved so as to strike the railroad in rear of the Union army,
along which all its supplies were conveyed from Chattanooga. Hood's
idea evidently was to interrupt all of Sherman's communications with
the North, and thus isolate him in the interior of Georgia, and force
him into a condition similar to that of Napoleon in his retreat from
Moscow. Grant, as has been heretofore explained, had never intended
to allow Sherman to be placed in this predicament; but had intended
him, after he arrived at Atlanta, to push on still farther, cutting loose
from all communication, as Grant himself had done at Vicksburg,
and striking for the sea, either at Mobile or Savannah, as might seem
preferable. Mobile, it was expected, would be the point; and, with
this view, Grant had early ordered Banks to attack and take Mobile,
so that he might be ready to meet Sherman, when the latter pushed
on in his interior march.

As soon, however, as it was apparent to Sherman that Hood
was attempting to interrupt the railroad line between Chattanooga
and Atlanta—especially when he saw that this was to be done with
an entire army—he proposed a modification of the plan to Grant.
Grant had intended Sherman to hold the line from Chattanooga to
Atlanta, but to cut loose entirely from the latter place; Sherman
suggested the destruction of Atlanta, and the entire abandonment of
the line from Atlanta to Chattanooga. Grant thought that, in this
event, Hood would strike for the North, and that even now he was
aiming at Middle Tennessee, while Sherman "would meet none but
old men, little boys, and railroad guards in his march through
Georgia;" but Sherman was positive that Hood would be forced to
turn and follow him. He thought Thomas, who was now in command
of Tennessee, would have no important enemy there. Grant still
insisted that Hood would avail himself of Sherman's absence to attack Thomas; but, after considering the matter a day, he sent the
required permission to Sherman, determining to collect reinforcements
so rapidly for Thomas, that that officer should be able to withstand
any rebel force which might be sent against him. The Government
was strongly in doubt about this whole movement, and even after
Grant had given Sherman authority for it, the general-in-chief was

telegraphed to reconsider once more. The Administration would not take the responsibility of prohibiting any military operation that Grant ordered, but it was anxious to show him how the movement was regarded at Washington. Grant, however, having once determined, was firm. He believed that Sherman would meet with no serious opposition, and that the moral effect of his march through the interior of the enemy's country, cutting the would-be Confederacy in two again, as had been done when the Mississippi was opened, would be prodigious. So the orders were not revoked, and Sherman began his preparations for the famous "march to the sea."

On the 14th of November, he had concentrated all the troops that Grant gave him for his movement, about seventy thousand men, at Atlanta. He would be obliged to subsist almost exclusively off of the enemy's country during his campaign, so that even an inferior force might compel him to head for such a point as he could reach, instead of one that he might prefer. No definite place where he was to come out was therefore fixed, but it was probable that it would be at Savannah or Mobile. Atlanta and its fortifications were now destroyed, and two corps of Sherman's army being sent back to reinforce Thomas, the railroad between Chattanooga and Atlanta was abandoned. Sherman was thus isolated, and started on his novel march. His condition was in many respects similar to Grant's after crossing the Mississippi, in the Vicksburg campaign, except in these two important particulars: Sherman's army was twice as large as Grant's had been, and Sherman had no enemy in his front, while Grant plunged in between two hostile armies, one of them greatly larger than his own.

THOMAS'S CAMPAIGN.

Grant now bent all his faculties to the task of preparing Thomas to defend himself against Hood, who, as the general-in-chief had foreseen, persisted in his northward and offensive campaign into Tennessee, leaving the South altogether open, and Sherman free to choose his route. "Had I had the power to command both armies," said Grant, "I should not have changed the orders under which Hood seemed to be acting." Every effort was made to reinforce Thomas before the rebel army could reach him; troops were withdrawn from Rosecranz, in Missouri, from A. J. Smith, who had belonged to the Red river expedition, under Banks, and recruits and men on furlough were hurried along every railroad from the North. By dint of immense exertions Thomas was reinforced sufficiently to be out of any extraordinary danger; and, although he fell back slowly before the advance of the enemy, he managed to detain the rebels till the 30th of November, at Franklin, where the main force of the Union army was posted, under Schofield, Thomas himself having fallen back still farther, to Nashville. Here the rebels attacked Schofield repeatedly, but were in every instance repulsed, losing one thousand seven hundred and fifty killed, seven hundred and two prisoners, and three thousand eight hundred wounded. Schofield's entire loss was only two thousand three hundred. During the night, under Thomas's orders, Schofield fell back to Nashville. This was solely in order to concentrate Thomas's whole force.

On the 15th of December, Hood, having approached still nearer to Nashville, Thomas attacked him, and, in a battle lasting two days, defeated and drove him from the field in utter confusion. Most of the rebel artillery, and many thousand prisoners, fell into the hands of Thomas. The enemy retreated at once, but was closely pursued with cavalry and infantry to the Tennessee, abandoning most of his artillery and transportation on the way. His army was almost completely annihilated.

CO-OPERATION ALL OVER THE CONTINENT.

Meanwhile, a combined naval and military expedition, planned by Grant against Fort Fisher the defence of Wilmington, at the mouth of the Cape Fear river, after meeting with various delays and hindrances, was crowned with complete success. This was a triumph of the utmost consequence. Wilmington was the last remaining place on the seacoast where the blockade maintained by the navy was ineffectual, and through this port supplies of inestimable value reached the interior. When this place was captured, the rebels were indeed shut in from the outside world; and the ever-contracting coils seemed folding closer and closer around the doomed and guilty disturbers of their country's peace.

Sherman had penetrated to Savannah by Christmas day, not a fortnight after the success of Thomas at Nashville. As Grant had foreseen, and foretold, he met no opposition of importance on the route; no battle was fought, and, in the occasional skirmishes with a small body of cavalry that hovered about his flanks, his outguards lost only a few hundred men. The campaign was one great excursion.

The country was found to be still abundant in supplies, though the railroads could no longer carry its productions to the armies at the rebel front. Sherman destroyed the railroads, the arsenals, bridges, and crops, everywhere on the route, and marked his course with a broad swath of ruin forty miles across. He reached the outworks of Savannah in five weeks after he had started, captured a fort that protected it without much difficulty, and was met at Savannah by fresh instructions from Grant, directing his future movements.

His march had been unique and interesting in the extreme. Certainly no great army ever marched before so far through an enemy's country and encountered so little opposition. Grant had heard of him by spies and deserters and through the rebel newspapers. He had been able to follow his march on the maps with very little anxiety, and had felt not half the solicitude for Sherman that the danger in which Thomas had been placed occasioned. He had actually started for Nashville, when the news of Thomas's brilliant success met him on the way, and relieved his fears.

Thomas had so completely placed Hood's army *hors du combat*, that Grant determined to find other fields of operation for his surplus troops. Some were sent to Canby, who had superseded Banks, and was ordered to organize the expedition against Mobile, which Grant had contemplated the year before; Schofield, with his entire corps, was ordered to be sent East, and the remainder of Thomas's available command was to be collected at Eastport, on the Tennessee. Schofield's movement, in the dead of winter, was difficult and painful in the extreme. On the 23d of January, his corps arrived at Washington, coming by rail through the snows and mountains of the Baltimore and Ohio road; then it was dispatched to Annapolis, to wait till the ice in Chesapeake bay would allow its transportation to the sea; for Grant intended to send Schofield into North Carolina to coöperate with Sherman.

The lieutenant general had at first thought to bring Sherman by sea from Savannah to City Point, and there, with the two great armies of the East and the West, to overwhelm the last remaining stronghold and army of the rebellion. Orders to this effect reached Sherman before he arrived at Savannah. He answered promptly that he had expected to march by land through the Carolinas, and thus join Grant, but that it would be at least six weeks after the fall of Savannah before he could reach Raleigh, in North Carolina; whereas by sea he could join Grant by the middle of January. He, therefore, began at once his preparations to obey Grant's orders. Grant, however, had before this discovered that the difficulty of procuring ocean transportation for a whole army would be prodigious, and he was, besides, pleased with Sherman's confidence of being able to march through the Carolinas. He, therefore, dispatched directions, on the 23th of December, for Sherman to start by land without delay, and march northward, through North and South Carolina, breaking up the railroads everywhere. This campaign was likely to be vastly more difficult and hazardous than that which Sherman had already accomplished, for now he would meet an enemy. There were still hostile troops on the seacoast south of Richmond, all of whom would be collected to oppose him, and Grant feared lest the remnants of Hood's army might be brought across from Mississippi, as a forlorn hope, in the last battles of the rebellion.

Accordingly, Schofield, with twenty-one thousand men, was sent to North Carolina, and instructed to take command of twelve thousand more, already there, at Newbern and Fort Fisher. He was then to move into the interior of the State, striking for Goldsboro, in order to reach Sherman at that point, as the latter should be coming North, and to furnish him with a new base of supplies. A vast accumulation of stores was also directed to be ready for the Western army when it should reach Goldsboro. Schofield captured Wilmington, and, after several skirmishes, which in any other war would be called battles, he reached a point ten miles from Cox's bridge, near Goldsboro, on the 22d of March, 1865.

Sherman left Savannah on the 1st of February, caused the evacuation of Charleston, seized Columbia, had a battle at Averysville, in which he was successful, and another at Bentonsville, where he encountered Johnston, who had been recently put in command of all the rebels that could be collected east of the Mississippi, and who were not under arms at Richmond. The engagement was not decisive, but Johnson retreated, and Sherman followed, till, on the 22d of March, he also arrived at Cox's bridge, which Schofield reached the same day, coming from the sea. Thus, one of the most wonderful pieces •of military combination that the world has ever seen, was accomplished under the orders, and according to the plans and instructions of Grant. A little more than four months previous, the general-in-chief had taken Schofield from Sherman's moving column, and ordered him back to the support of Thomas, in Tennessee. At the same time that he brought Schofield north from Atlanta, he sent Sherman south into the inmost penetraliá of the rebellion. The latter had reached the Atlantic, and then marched north, capturing cities and fighting enemies all through the balmy region of the Carolinas. Schofield had fought and won the batte of Franklin, had borne a distinguished part in the battle of Nashville, and then brought his corps through snows and ice across the continent in mid-winter, to the Atlantic coast, sailed to North Carolina, captured Wilmington, and advanced into the interior of the State, to rejoin and support his old commander. Between them, they had nearly traversed the whole interior region in rebellion. Each arrived on the same day at Goldsboro, having traversed thousands of miles. No general ever conceived or executed such a combination as this, prior to Grant, and yet you shall hear ignorant or hostile critics tell us that his success is owing to luck. The magnificent scale of his operations; the closeness with which he followed and directed them all; the complicated nature of his various evolutions under a dozen different commanders; the marvellous skill with which he was able to make Sherman march south and Schofield north; to get reinforcements to Thomas from Canby and Rosecranz, at the critical moment, so as to secure the great triumph of the battle of Nashville; to capture Fort Fisher and Wilmington, although at extraordinary risk and after peculiar difficulties, just in time for those captures to afford immense assistance to other schemes; subsequently, to bring Sherman north and to send Schofield south; while, all the while, he himself was holding the main force and greatest army of the rebellion, not only at bay, but in terror for its existence—this fact alone rendering all the operations of his subordinates possible;—all this maybe luck, but it is such luck as never followed any soldier before in history; it is such luck as it is greatly to be desired shall always attend the armies of the Republic; it is such luck as nations have always recognized, securing for themselves the advantages it brings, by placing its possessors in civil as well as military power. If the same luck will only attend the administration of President Grant, which marked his career as general-in-chief, the country will be satisfied.

One beautiful and magnanimous trait of Grant deserves to be chronicled here. While he assigned to his subordinates all these brilliant and important parts of his plans, and retained for himself not only the most difficult, but the least inspiring of all, he never manifested a particle of jealousy at the reputation which he enabled Sherman, and Sheridan, and Thomas, and Schofield, and Terry to acquire. Not only did he urge upon the Government the promotion of those officers, as well as of Meade, but he sought every other means to bring them into notice. His wonderful sagacity was manifest in detecting not only their ability, when nobody else perceived it, but in recognizing the peculiar quality of each man's talent; the original genius of Sherman, which fitted him for the great march; the brilliant vigor of Sheridan, which enabled him to conquer Early; the splendid determination of Thomas, which alone retarded Hood until the hour had come for his annihilation; the sagacity of Schofield, the talent of Terry. But, more than all this, when he had lain many weary months in front of Peters-burg, making movements all of which tended gradually to his eventual success, but none of which resulted so immediately in what the country desired as to be recognized by the country; while he was in reality conceiving and inspiring and directing every one of his great subordinates, he never sought to take from them an atom of their own glory; nor even when the ignorant bestowed on the executor all the praise, did the conceiver and controller attempt to attribute to himself his own. He was calm, patient, unselfish, magnanimous. He was not anxious for fame, but for the salvation of the country. When Sherman penetrated to the Atlantic coast, and accomplished his won-derful march, Grant, who had conceived the idea of that march, and taken all of its responsibility, was still sitting quietly in front of Petersburg; and the country rang with applause for the brilliant lieu-tenant, affording no share of this to the chief who had sent the lieuten-ant on his errand, and by his other movements, a thousand miles away, had rendered the success of the lieutenant possible. It was even proposed in Congress to place Sherman in the rank which Grant enjoyed. Sherman wrote on the subject at once to Grant, saying that the proposition was without his knowledge, and begging Grant to use his influence against it. This, of course, Grant refused to do, and replied to Sherman, "*If you are put above me, I shall always obey you, just as you always have me.*" The history of the world may be searched in vain to find a parallel of magnanimity, friendship, and patriotism.

In January, 1865, foreseeing the approaching termination of the war, and anxious to make the downfall of the rebellion complete, Grant directed Thomas to send out several expeditions into the region between the Alleghanies and the Mississippi, in order to accomplish the destruction of all the remaining resources and communications of the enemy. Stoneman was sent from East Tennessee into South Caro-lina, to attract all attention from Sherman in his northward march, and Wilson was to be ordered into central Alabama, which was now entirely exposed and unprotected. Canby also, who was in command of everything in the region of the extreme southwest, was directed to organize an expedition against Mobile, and Sheridan received orders to move from the valley towards Lynchburg, in the rear of Lee, so as to destroy every possible means by which the last of the great rebel armies could draw their supplies. Thus, from every direction, raids were being made at and into the vitals of the rebellion, while Grant still held the main army in his front unable to attack him, but equally unable to move to the protection of the threatened points. His plans had annihilated all of the resources of the enemy; his subordinates had attacked all the important outside points, his movements had conquered all the rebel armies but one, and now he was ready to deal the death-blow for which he and the nation had been waiting so long. Now, at last, the country began to perceive the consummate nature of his strategy; now it began to recognize the master in the movements of his subordinates; now it detected the unity of his plans, discovering that Sherman and Sheridan and Schofield and Thomas were moving towards one centre, and that that centre was Grant; that they were all inspired by one mind, and that that mind was Grant's. The rebels, also, too plainly saw and felt, for the first time, that they had a master; they turned and writhed, they showed a bold front, but they were aware that the hour had come, that their schemes had been met by counter schemes; that they were outgeneralled, outmanœuvred, outmarched, outfought, outwitted, conquered, although the final blow was not yet struck.

In March, Grant ordered Sherman, who had now reached Goldsboro, to come in person to City Point, and receive verbal instructions. Before Sherman arrived, Sheridan had completely destroyed all the canals and railroads to the northwest of Lee, and was ordered to bring his whole force to Grant, who now directed Sherman to prevent any concentration between Lee and Johnston, and to be ready to come to the support of Grant, if the latter should so instruct. Sherman spent a day at City Point, and returned to his command.

On the 29th of March, Sheridan having arrived in front of Petersburg, Grant began the final campaign of the war. On the 25th, Lee had made an assault on Grant's lines, which must have been a mere frantic stroke, such as a dying beast gives in the arena, with no hope of success, but simply to glut its rage. It was promptly repelled, the enemy losing heavily in killed and wounded, and Grant capturing two thousand prisoners. Grant immediately took advantage of this, and made a counter advance on the left, which was successful, nearly a thousand more rebels being captured, and many others killed and wounded, and a portion of Lee's line taken and held. Grant had been extremely anxious for months lest the enemy should withdraw from Richmond and Petersburg. He was unwilling to move in attack with the Army of the Potomac until his great plans for the entire continent should be further consummated; until Sherman and Schofield could be brought so near, on their converging lines, that Lee could have no chance of escape, even if he attempted it; but now all things were ripened, every command was in its right place; from all directions he had brought his armies, and, on the 29th of March, he moved.

Leaving a force of twenty or thirty thousand in the lines in front of Petersburg and Richmond, he extended his left with the view of overlapping the rebel right and seizing the South-Side road. His moving force now was between ninety thousand and one hundred thousand strong. Lee still, by superhuman exertions, had collected seventy thousand men, besides the local militia of Richmond, and the gunboat crews on the James, which, together, amounted to at least five thousand more, and which were always put into a fight by the rebel general. Grant left so large a force in front of the rebel works, in order that, if the enemy should be induced to come out and attack the national column while in motion, the troops in the trenches might be pushed at once and without further orders against the fortifications in their fronts. Sheridan, Grant detached and sent to the extreme left, to be ready to cut and cross the two southern railroads which Lee still retained; the South-Side and the Danville. With the remainder of his force, Grant then moved to the left for the last time, and began to feel the enemy. He soon discovered that Lee was still confronting him at every point, and conceived, therefore, that the rebel line must be weakly held. He determined, in consequence, to move no farther out, but to send a corps of infantry to Sheridan, who was still on the extreme left, so that he might turn the enemy's right flank, while with the rest of the force Grant would order a direct assault on the rebel line. Meantime, Lee had not yet lost all spirit; he hoped still to gain some advantage, under cover of which he could join Johnston, when the two armies might perhaps be able to make a campaign against Grant's united forces in the interior. Accordingly, one or two feeble attacks were made by Lee, but immediately repelled with loss. In these various operations, Sheridan was separated from Grant's left, with a view to making the contemplated flank attack on Lee; and the rebel commander discovering this, immediately reinforced his own right largely, and moved against Sheridan. And now Sheridan displayed great generalship. Instead of retreating upon Grant with his whole command, to tell the story of having encountered superior force, he deployed his cavalry on foot, leaving mounted men only to take charge of the horses. This skillful ruse compelled the enemy also to deploy over a vast extent of woods and broken country, and made his progress slow. Sheridan now informed Grant of what had taken place, and Grant promptly reinforced him with the Fifth corps. On the 1st of April, thus reinforced, Sheridan attacked Lee's right at Five Forks, assaulted and carried the fortified position of the enemy, capturing all his artillery, and between five thousand and six thousand prisoners. The defeat was decisive. The rebels fled in every direction, and the bulk of the force that had been in front of Sheridan never was able again to rejoin Lee.

News of the victory reached Grant at nine o'clock in the evening. He at once determined that the hour had come for the final assault. Without consulting any one, he wrote a dispatch to Meade, ordering an attack at midnight, all along the lines in front of Petersburg, which were at least ten miles long. When one remembers the numerous assaults upon fortified places that had been made during the war, and their frequently disastrous results; the immense strength of the works of Petersburg, which the rebels had now been nearly a year in elaborating, and whose terrible excellence Grant had tested so often; the prejudice in the country against such assaults, and the possibility of repulse; how much was at stake at this crisis, of life and fame; how, perhaps, the very termination of the war might depend on the success of this assault;—the moral courage of the man who ordered it can be better appreciated. But his courage never failed when his judgment was decided. He had been able to wait patiently through the long and tedious months of the siege, to withstand the impatience of the country, the entreaties of the Government, the weariness of the soldiers, and, perhaps, the promptings of ambition—all of which required fortitude of the most determined sort; but now he was to evince that species of courage which amounts to audacity, and which, · when successful, becomes sublime. As soon as he was certain of Sheridan's complete success, he was also certain of what he himself wanted to do. With an intuition of both intellect and of feeling, he saw that the opportunity had arrived, and was confident that his

8

men would be as much inspired by the victory at Five Forks as the
rebels must be disheartened. He had no fears that the famous lines
would not be carried at last. The news of Five Forks was sent all
along the army, night though it was, and preparations were made for
the assault. The corps commanders, however, could not be ready
until dawn, and it was therefore postponed to that time. Before daylight a prodigious bombardment was begun, and at four o'clock the
various columns moved to the assault. Grant's calculations were correct; the rebel works were carried in three different places. Lee's
army was cut in two or three parts; many instantly fled across the
Appomattox, while the main portion retreated into the city of Petersburg, which was still defended by an inner line. Grant got his men up
from the extended field which they now occupied, and pursued the
rebels into the town; several thousand prisoners and many guns were
taken before dark.

That night the enemy evacuated Petersburg and Richmond, flying
southwest towards Danville. So the goal that our armies had been
four years seeking to attain was won. Grant did not wait a moment,
but, without entering Richmond in person, pushed on in pursuit at daylight, on the 3d, leaving to a subordinate the glory of seizing the
capital of Virginia. The energy with which he now followed the un-
happy Lee was terrific; he disposed his columns on two roads, and
marched with marvellous speed. Sheridan, Ord, Meade, vied with
each other in their efforts to overtake and annihilate the last fighting
force of the rebellion; and the men, inspired with their recent and
magnificent triumphs, murmured at no labors or dangers. Meanwhile, mindful, even at this intense crisis, of all other and coöperative
emergencies, Grant, as he was pursuing Lee, sent orders to Sherman
to push at once against Johnston, so that the war might be finished at
once. " Rebel armies," he reminded him, "are now the only strategic
points to strike at." Sheridan, with the Sixth corps, came up with
Lee, on the 6th, at Sailor's creek, struck the enemy in force, and captured sixteen pieces of artillery and seven thousand prisoners, among
whom were seven generals. Ord also engaged the enemy on this day
at Farmville. And thus the remorseless conqueror went on, pursuing and striking his enemy by turns. Every day Lee made superhuman exertions to get beyond the pursuer's reach; every day he found
himself circumvented, outmanœuvred, or beaten down again. No time
was left him to get supplies; his men were subsisting on two ears of
corn a piece per day, and the arrangements he sought to make to

procure them rations, were discovered and frustrated by Grant. A train of cars loaded with supplies was captured by Sheridan, and a wagon-train with rations was set on fire by artillery.

On the 7th of April, Grant addressed a note to Lee, summoning him to surrender; but Lee sought to gain time, either hoping yet to reach Johnston with some fragments of his army, or at least to allow Johnston an opportunity to escape. So he diplomatized, and was willing to make peace; but Grant was not to be outwitted, and though he continued the correspondence, ceased not his advance or his blows. Lee said he was not certain the emergency had arisen to call for his surrender; whereupon Sheridan was thrown around in front of Lee, and drove him from Appomattox, capturing twenty-five pieces of artillery. This, probably, rendered Lee less uncertain about the emergency. But Grant declined entirely to treat for peace; all he wanted was surrender. He now sent the Twenty-Fourth corps, under Ord, and the Fifth, under Griffin, to support Sheridan, thus completely surrounding Lee, who was fairly outmarched; Sheridan was planted square across his only road of escape. The great cavalryman at once began to attack Lee, who, at first believing there was no infantry in his front, endeavored to drive Sheridan away; but suddenly discovering the presence of two corps of infantry, which he had not deemed it possible could have marched fast enough to pass his own troops flying under the impulse of terror, he at once sent word to Sheridan that he was negotiating with Grant.

APPOMATTOX.

On the 9th of April, Lee asked for an interview with the commander of the Union armies, for the purpose of surrendering his forces, and early in the afternoon of that memorable day, the two antagonists met in a plain farm-house, between the armies which had striven against each other so long.

Lee had a solitary staff officer with him, and with Grant were about a dozen of his subordinates—Sheridan, Ord, and his own staff. And then and there, and in this presence, Grant drew up the terms upon which Lee surrendered. Grant first announced what he should dedemand, and Lee acquiesced. No one else spoke on the subject. Grant then wrote out the stipulations; they were copied by staff officers; Lee signed them, and the Army of Northern Virginia was prisoner of war. The terms are world renowned: "Officers and men were parolod, and allowed to return to their homes, not to be disturbed by United States authority so long as they observed their paroles and the laws in force where they might reside." All arms, artillery, and public property were to be turned over to officers appointed by Grant. These were the stipulations, as Lee consented to them; but after he had signified his acceptance, Grant inserted the clause that the side-arms and private horses and baggage of the officers might be retained. Lee seemed much gratified at this magnanimity, which saved him and his officers the peculiar humiliation of a formal surrender of their weapons. He asked, how about the horses of the cavalry *men*, which in the rebel army were the property of the private soldier? Grant replied that these were included in the surrender. Lee looked at the paper again, and acquiesced in Grant's interpretation. The latter then said, "*I will not change the terms of the surrender, General Lee,* BUT I WILL INSTRUCT MY OFFICERS, WHO RECEIVE THE PAROLES, TO ALLOW THE MEN TO RETAIN THEIR HORSES, AND TAKE THEM HOME TO WORK THEIR LITTLE FARMS." Again General Lee expressed his appreciation of the generosity of his conqueror, and declared that he thought this liberality would have a very good effect. So the interview terminated.

The next day, Grant and Lee met again on horseback, in the open air, and for two hours discussed the situation of affairs. Lee ex-pressed a great desire for peace, believed that his surrender was the end of the war; he acquiesced in the abolition of slavery, the return of the seceded States, and declared his wish for harmony. Grant urged him to use his influence to bring about such a result. Subsequently, on the same day, Longstreet, Gordon, Heth, Pickett, Wilcox, W. H. F. Lee, and every other officer of high rank in Lee's army, came in a body to pay their respects to Grant, and, as they themselves expressed it, to thank him for the terms he had allowed him. All manifested the kindest spirit. Many of Grant's officers were present at this remarkable interview, and not a word was said on either side calcu-lated to wound the feelings of any one present. Many of the rebels declared how unwillingly they had entered the war; all submitted fully to the inevitable; many expected to be exiled; none dreamed of retaining any property; they expected all their lands to be confiscated, and themselves to begin life all over again. As for political power, the man who had mentioned it would have been scouted at, for insulting them. They said they had staked all and lost, and they were grateful to retain even their lives; while the unexampled delicacy that had left them their swords, the pledge to a soldier of his military honor, touched their proud hearts deeply, and they were too proud not to acknowledge it.

Had it been in the power of the men who visited Grant at Appomattox on that day to speak for the South, none of the difficulties that have since occurred would have disturbed this land. Grant, however, is destined to yet another victory, over such of them as have since returned to their ancient and defiant spirit, and over all their adherents, North and South; and after another Appomattox at the polls, they will be as ready to accept his terms as before. And this time, he will remain where he can administer the fruits of the victories in the field and at the ballot-box, which he will have achieved. Knowing this, and having felt his sword, these men will *remain* submissive; and, trusting again to his magnanimity, which also they experienced before, they will not find their trust in vain. He and those whom he represents will disarm them, and render them powerless for further mischief to their country; but desire no spoliation, no humiliation, no needless suffering of their foes. The results which these men looked for at Appomattox, and which Grant there conquered by his skill and the matchless endurance of his soldiers, will thus be secured forever, and a true Union, under the sway of Union-loving men, perpetuated.

On the day of this wonderful meeting, Grant started for Washington. He was well aware that the war was closed. He knew that after the surrender of Lee and the capture of Richmond, no other rebel force would remain in arms, and he was anxious at once to proceed to lessen the expenditures of the Government, and to muster out his soldiers. He hastened from Appomattox to City Point, everywhere on the route the inhabitants coming out " to see the man who had whipped Lee." Then, without even yet stopping to enter the capital that he had conquered, or the lines that had withstood him so long; without apparently a particle of the natural and pardonable self-glorification of a victor under such extraordinary circumstances, this man, as modest in triumph as he had been persistent in difficulty, and sagacious in council, and daring in danger, went on to Washington, to engage in the unobtrusive, but still vastly important duties of retrenchment.

SUMMARY.

In this concluding and most glorious of all the campaigns of the war, Grant had lost seven thousand men, in killed, wounded, and missing. He had captured Petersburg and Richmond, and won, by his subordinates, the battles of Five Forks and Sailor's Creek, besides numerous smaller ones; he had broken the lines at Petersburg in three several places, captured twenty thousand men in actual battle, and received the surrender of twenty-seven thousand others at Appomattox, and absolutely annihilated an army of seventy thousand soldiers. Ten thousand, at least, of Lee's army deserted on the road from Richmond to Appomattox, and at least ten thousand more were killed or wounded. From Lee's own field-return, now on file in the War Office, we learn his force at the beginning of the campaign. Such an absolute annihilation of an army never occurred before, in so short a time, in the history of the world.

On the 29th of March, Richmond was in the possession of the rebels; their *de facto* government was established and recognized over hundreds of thousands of miles; the forces of Lee lined fifty miles of works that defended Petersburg and the capital; their greatest commander was at the head of seventy thousand veterans. In less than two weeks, Richmond and Petersburg were captured cities, the lines that had defended them so long were useless, except as trophies of the humiliation of those who built them; their government, so called, was a fugitive, with "none so poor to do it reverence;" their army was not only defeated, but stricken out of existence; its general, and every man under him who had not been killed, was a prisoner of war. Twenty-seven thousand soldiers never before surrendered *in the open field, behind no works, without a siege.* As purely military events, these are unparalleled.

This last campaign was so short, that its history was hardly reported at the time, and its results were so stupendous, that its own amazing character has hardly yet been recognized. For splendid marching, for repeated and victorious battles, for capture of works thought to be impregnable, for vigor and rapidity of movement, and remorseless energy, it will compare favorably with any achievements of ancient or modern times.

The total loss during the entire year, among the troops immediately under Grant, including those commanded by Butler in the first month of the campaign, amounted to twelve thousand six hundred and ninety-five killed, forty-seven thousand eight hundred and twenty-two wounded, and twenty thousand four hundred and ninety-eight missing; total, eighty-two thousand seven hundred and twenty. Against this, it is impossible to set off an exact statement of the losses of the enemy, for no reports were ever made by the rebels of the final battles of the war. There was no one to whom to report. But Grant captured alone, sixty-six thousand five hundred and twelve rebel soldiers in that time, besides the killed or wounded. He absolutely annihilated every army opposed to him; that of Lee, that of Early, of Beauregard, and all the forces brought from West Virginia and North and South Carolina to reinforce Lee; leaving not a living man at the last of all those armies who was not a prisoner. So that, with forces not a fourth greater than those of his antagonist, and in spite of the enormous advantages of defensive breastworks everywhere enjoyed by that antagonist, and which far more than balanced Grant's superiority in numbers, he accomplished military results that for completeness are utterly without precedent.

RETRENCHMENT.

Thus ended the greatest civil war in history. Lee surrendered on the 9th of April, and on the 13th Grant was back in Washington, and at once urged upon the President and the Secretary of War that, as the rebellion was a thing of the past, the work of cutting down the military expenses of the Government should begin; accordingly, on the day of his arrival at the capital, the following announcement was made to the country :

"WAR DEPARTMENT, WASHINGTON,
"*April* 13, 6 P. M.

"The Department, after mature consideration and *consultation with the Lieutenant General* upon the results of the recent campaign, has come to the following determinations, which will be carried into effect by appropriate orders, to be immediately issued :

"First, to stop all drafting and recruiting in the loyal States.

"Second, to curtail purchases for arms, ammunition, quartermaster, and commissary supplies, and reduce the military establishment in its several branches.

"Third, to reduce the number of general and staff officers to the actual necessities of the service.

"Fourth, to remove all military restrictions upon trade and commerce, so far as may be consistent with public safety."

ASSASSINATION OF PRESIDENT LINCOLN.

These important reductions in expenditure announced to the nation the absolute overthrow of the rebellion and the return to peace. The enthusiasm natural over the immense success that had been gained, at once broke out all over the land. In Washington, a great illumination of all the public and many private buildings took place, and on the 14th of April, the day after Grant's return, it was announced in the public journals that he would accompany the President that evening to Ford's Theatre; but Grant had not seen his children for several months, and had a distaste for public demonstrations. He therefore declined the President's invitation, and started on the evening of the 14th for Burlington, New Jersey, where his children were at school. Thus, fortunately for America, did Providence again direct the movements of her greatest captain, and preserved him in peace, as it had done in war, for the future emergencies which he was destined to control. That night, as is too well known in the history of the country, the President was assassinated at the theatre. It was clearly proven, in the proceedings of the trial, that the conspirators intended also to take the life of him who had so recently preserved the life of the country. The crime, however, was not permitted by Heaven; the attempted visit to Burlington took Grant unexpectedly out of the reach of the assassin's blow. The Secretary of War at once telegraphed to the general-in-chief, who returned the same night to Washington, having got no farther than Philadelphia.

This extraordinary and melancholy event, and the novelty of the arrangements which it imposed on the Government, retained Grant in Washington for several days. The funeral of the President took place on the 19th of April; his successor, Andrew Johnson, having been inaugurated immediately upon the death of Mr. Lincoln, on the 15th.

SHERMAN'S TERMS.

In obedience to Grant's order, of the 5th of April, to "push on from where you are, and let us see if we cannot finish the job with Lee's and Johnston's armies," Sherman had moved at once against Johnston, who retreated rapidly before him through Raleigh, which Sherman entered on the 13th. The day preceding, news had reached him of the surrender of Lee. On the 14th, a correspondence was opened between Sherman and Johnston, which resulted, on the 18th, in an agreement for a suspension of hostilities, and a memorandum or basis for peace, subject, of course, to the approval of the President. The memorandum was forwarded first to Grant, who immediately perceived that the terms were such as the country would not consent to, as they allowed the rebels to deposit their arms and public property in the several State arsenals, stipulated for the recognition of the rebel State governments by the authorities at Washington, secured to the rebels, without exception, all their political rights and franchises, as well as their rights of person and property, and, in fact, announced a complete and absolute amnesty, simply on condition of the disbandment of the rebel armies, the distribution of arms, and the resumption of peaceful pursuits by those who composed those armies Nothing was said about the abolition of slavery, the right of secession, punishment of past treason, or security against future rebellion. Grant forwarded the papers to the Secretary of War, and asked that a Cabinet meeting might be called at once, to determine what action should be taken, for there was no time to lose. Grant received Sherman's dispatches on the evening of the 20th, and the Cabinet meeting was called before midnight. Grant was present.

The President and his Secretaries were unanimous in condemning the action of Sherman; indeed, their language was so strong, that Grant, while agreeing fully with them that the terms were inadmissible, yet felt it his duty to his friend to defend his conduct from the imputations it excited. He declared that the services Sherman had rendered the country for more than four years entitled him to the most lenient judgment on his act, and proved that whatever might be said of his opinions, his motives were unquestioned. The President was especially indignant at Sherman's course, and the sympathy for rebels which it was thought to reveal.

Grant was instructed to start at once for Raleigh, and assume command in person, revoking the terms, and thereafter take whatever action he thought fit. He started before daybreak of the 21st, and arrived at Raleigh on the 24th. There he informed Sherman, as delicately as possible, of the disapproval of his memorandum, and directed him to exact from Johnston the same terms which had been granted to Lee. Sherman was thoroughly subordinate, and at once notified Johnston that their arrangement had been disapproved; and a second set of stipulations was drawn up, in conformity with Grant's instructions. Grant, however, magnanimously kept himself in the background; he was not present at any interview with Johnston, remaining at Raleigh while Sherman went out to the front; and his name does not appear in the papers, except where, after the signatures of Sherman and Johnston, he wrote, "Approved: U. S. Grant." This the rebel commander was not aware of, and Grant actually went back to Washington without Johnston's suspecting that he had been at Raleigh. He allowed Sherman to receive the surrender, although he could, in compliance with the especial authority and orders given him in Washington, have had the glory of accepting the capitulation of Johnston, as well as that of Lee. What other living man would have been capable of such self-abnegation? and yet, how infinitely greater the glory of declining! One hardly knows which to admire most, at this supreme crisis in the history of the country and of the man—the magnanimity manifested to his enemy at Appomattox, or the generosity displayed to his friend at Raleigh.

Grant went immediately back to Washington, taking care everywhere to defend Sherman; throwing around his friend the shield of his own great reputation, and assuring everybody that Sherman's loyalty was as unquestioned as his own. The indignation throughout the land was intense, and nothing but Grant's own splendid fame, and the persistency with which he fought for Sherman, saved that illustrious soldier from insult, and perhaps degradation.

On the 28th of April, Grant was again at his headquarters, now established at Washington, and the same day orders were issued for the reduction of the forces in the field and garrison, and the expenses of every department in the army. These orders effected an immediate diminution of expense to the amount of hundreds of millions of dollars.

The various expeditions of Stoneman, Wilson, and Canby had meanwhile accomplished all that they were sent to do. There was no force of consequence left in front of either of them. Canby took possession of Mobile on the 11th of April, Wilson roamed unmolested and almost unopposed through the interior of Alabama, until he was arrested by the news of the surrender of Lee, and Stoneman had a similar career in North Carolina. But as soon as the various rebel forces, large or small, heard of the disasters of Johnston and Lee, and the terms accorded to them, they also made haste to offer themselves as candidates for the same mercy extended to their comrades. During the month of May, the last armies of any strength left to the rebellion, those under Dick Taylor and Kirby Smith, surrendered on the same terms, and, by the 1st of June, not an armed rebel remained in the land.

THE COLLAPSE.

The collapse of the revolt was one of the most astounding features connected with the war. Not a gun was fired in hostility after the surrender of Lee. Not a soldier held out; not even a guerilla remained in arms; none retreated to a mountain fastness; none hesitated not only to give a parole, but to volunteer an oath of allegiance to the Government they had offended. Great part of this wonderful acquiescence in the results of the war was owing to the magnanimity of the terms accorded by Grant. No greater stroke of statesmanship can be found recorded in history. Knowing, as he did, the exhausted condition of the rebels;—aware that they could hope for no after success, and yet might prolong the fighting for a year in the interior, with small detachments; partizan bands, holding out here and there all over the country; collecting together as fast as they were separated; renewing the fight after they seemed subdued;—he determined to grant them such terms that there would be neither object nor excuse left them for such a course. The consummate wisdom of his conduct was proved by the haste which the rebels made to yield everything they had fought for. They were ready not only to give up arms, but, as has been said, to swear fidelity to the Government. They acquiesced in the abolition of slavery, they abandoned the heresy of secession, and waited in humility to see what else their conquerors would dictate. And they did this in excellent spirit. They said they had staked all, and lost all; they admitted it was fair that the Government should treat them as conquered rebels; they were thankful for their lives; they did not know if their lands would be left them; they dreamed not of political power; they did not hope to vote; they only asked to be let live quietly under the flag they had outraged, and attempt in some slight degree to build up their shattered fortunes. Many did not scruple to say that they would be better off now than if the rebellion had succeeded; many openly declared they were even more likely to prosper than during the days when the rebellion had existed. Some announced that they were glad that the war had ended as it did, and were proud to be back again under the Government under which they had been born. The greatest general of the rebellion asked for pardon.

GRATITUDE TO GRANT.

All proclaimed especially their admiration of Grant's generosity. General Lee refused to present his petition for amnesty until he had ascertained in advance that Grant would recommend it. Mrs. Jefferson Davis wrote to Grant, and went in person to see him, asking his all-powerful influence to obtain a remission of some of the punishment of her husband; and throughout the South his praises were on the lips of his conquered foes.

If this was so at the South, the North awarded him such a unanimity of praise and affection as no American had ever received before. Houses were furnished and presented to him, in Philadelphia, Washington, and Galena; magnificent donations of money were placed at his disposal; whenever he stepped out of his house, crowds attended and applauded him; at every public place, theatre or church, the audience or congregation rose at his entrance. If he visited a town, the mayor and other authorities welcomed him; cities were illuminated because of his presence, processions were formed in his honor, and the whole summer of 1865 was one long ovation. The nation felt that it could not do enough for the man who had led its armies to victory; men of every shade of political, religious, and social opinion or position, united in these acclamations.

But amid them all Grant preserved a modesty as remarkable as the ability which had won them. He made a tour of several months through the Northern States, during which probably every distinguished man in the country, besides innumerable crowds of less illustrious, but quite as hearty and patriotic friends, combined to do him honor; and in all this period, his quiet, unobtrusive manner, his simplicity of speech and dress, his equanimity and modesty, were as much admired as his deeds. To see him, one would never have suspected that the parade and celebration were on his account. He never spoke of his achievements or his success; he never alluded to the demonstrations in his honor; he accepted and appreciated the kindness that was offered him, thanked the people in the simplest and plainest terms, and won their love, where before he had only their admiration and their gratitude.

PRESIDENTIAL RECONSTRUCTION.

So passed the summer away. Meanwhile, the President had been endeavoring to reconstruct the Union. Upon the assassination of Mr. Lincoln, there had been great fears entertained by all moderate men, that the harshness of Andrew Johnson and his revengeful violence towards the rebels would postpone for a long time any real harmony. He had openly announced his belief that all traitors should be hanged, and had threatened what severities he would use, if he were President of the United States. Grant himself was sincerely anxious on this matter. The extreme violence of the President, when discussing Sherman's terms to the rebels, increased this anxiety, and at first it seemed as if it was destined to have ample cause. The President denounced the rebels bitterly, he refused to pardon any, he kept many civilians imprisoned, he was determined, he said, "to render treason odious;" he was anxious to try and to punish even those whom Grant had paroled.

Repeatedly, when Grant was summoned to Cabinet meetings, the President wanted to know when the time would come that Lee and other paroled officers could be tried and punished; and Grant was obliged to intercede and defend them. He maintained that the paroles protected them; that they could not be tried while they obeyed the laws and complied with the stipulations they had entered into. He was obliged more than once to be very emphatic on this point. He thought we had received a very good equivalent for the lives of a few leaders, by securing all their arms and getting themselves under our control, bound by their oaths to obey the law; and, having received this consideration, he held that we ourselves were bound in honor to maintain them in theirs.*

MAGNANIMITY OF GRANT.

As has been seen, Grant early recommended the pardon of General Lee, on the ground that it would do much to secure harmony; and favored that of General Johnston, because of the excellent tone and spirit he had displayed. Indeed, when measures were taken by a subordinate of the Government in Virginia, to bring General Lee to trial, that officer at once appealed to Grant, to know if he thought the terms at Appomattox allowed this. Grant insisted that they did not, and so informed Lee; and went in person to the President on the subject, besides stating his views officially and in writing; and the proceedings were stopped. So, also, he sought to alleviate some of the sufferings of Jefferson Davis in his prison at Fort Monroe; but in this he was not so successful. He never lost a chance to show a magnanimous spirit to his fallen foes; and, owing to the feeling of the President, these chances were constant and numerous. So it came about that the South looked to Grant especially, as their guardian and protector against Andrew Johnson.

But, as time wore on, the enmity of the President towards those who had been rebels was modified. They made haste to subscribe

---

*See Grant's testimony before Judiciary Committee.

to his terms; whatever he told them to do they did, and, pleased
with this, he flattered himself that he alone could reconstruct the
Union. He appointed governors without a shadow of law; he exacted changes in the constitutions of the seceded States; he established a policy—all without the sanction of Congress, which was not
in session, and had no power to summon itself, and which he persistently refused to call together, lest it should obstruct his policy; so
that, by the 1st of December, when Congress by law assembled, he
had built up an elaborate system of reconstruction, for which neither
the Constitution nor the laws of the land could afford a particle of
authority. It was true, the times were revolutionary, but his acts
were autocratic and still more revolutionary, subversive of every
democratic principle, assuming to himself powers more extraordinary
than any potentate in Europe ventures to-day to exercise. He could
easily have called the Congress and consulted with them, and, if they
differed with him, he was but the executive and they the legislative,
the *law-making* power of the Government. The Constitution itself
prescribes that the President shall simply *execute* the laws made by
Congress.

OPPOSITION OF CONGRESS.

But Congress met, and it was at once apparent that his scheme
was not approved by either house. He had not taken nor exacted
the guarantees which Congress insisted were necessary from those
lately in rebellion. He was willing to admit them at once to a full
share in the Government; Congress thought measures should be taken
to secure what had been won by the war. He seemed willing to withdraw the military from the South ; Congress wished it to be retained.
He would permit those who had been prominent in treason to retain
that prominence in the rescued Government; Congress was unwilling
for this. He made no provision for the protection and elevation of
the emancipated millions; Congress thought this was one of the first
duties of the nation.

Grant took no part in the contest between the two divisions of the
Government. He was purely a military officer, and unwilling to
obtrude himself into civil affairs. He was anxious for perfect harmony and peace to be reëstablished throughout the land, and inclined
to the most lenient treatment of the rebels, consistent with retaining
the advantages that had been so dearly bought. And although he
was not consulted in the policy originated by the President, yet, as

the latter did not choose to call Congress together, and as it was necessary to construct some system, he acquiesced when the President enunciated his plan. But he always thought and said, that whatever the President did must be provisional; he held that Congress, the representative of the people, must eventually decide what the law should be, and to its decision all must bow.

GRANT'S SOUTHERN TOUR.

In November, before Congress had assembled, the President sent Grant to make a tour through the South, and to report upon the condition of affairs. He returned in about three weeks, having visited Richmond, North and South Carolina, Georgia, and Tennessee. Everywhere he was received with great respect by the people whom he had conquered. The governors and mayors instantly called to pay him their respects, the State legislatures invited him to their chambers and rose in form to greet him, addresses were made him, and though there was no enthusiasm, there was a decided cordiality. In private, many of the most prominent civilians and generals of the rebellion called on him.

His report to the President was dated December 18, 1865. It stated that "the mass of thinking men of the South accept the situation of affairs in good faith." Slavery and the right of secession they had entirely abandoned; and some of their leading men even declared that the result of the war was fortunate. Grant recommended, however, that a strong military force should still be retained at the South, although he believed that "the citizens of that region were anxious to return to self-government within the Union as soon as possible." There is no doubt that this is exactly the condition of affairs which existed at the South at that time, and that, if this spirit had been fostered, the rebels would have submitted promptly to the conditions which before long Congress imposed.

THE RUPTURE.

But in February, the quarrel between the President and Congress came to an open breach. Grant had striven hard to prevent this; he felt the necessity of harmony between these two branches of the Government at this important crisis, and went from one to another, using the immense weight and influence which his achievements gave him,

to heal the discord. Many Congressmen, also, were extremely unwilling to come to a rupture with the President whom they had elected.
But Mr. Johnson was determined that his policy should prevail, and
would listen to no overtures from Congress in which this was not
stipulated. Congress, however, especially insisted that those who had
been leaders in the rebellion should be disqualified from holding office,
and that the principle of representation in Congress from the southern
States should be changed. Hitherto, before the war, and during the
existence of slavery, members of the lower House had been chosen,
not only one for every certain number of inhabitants, but also one for
every certain number of slaves, though the slaves had no votes; so
that the vote of a white man at the South was worth nearly half as
much again as that of a white man at the North. One vote at the
South did half as much again to elect a Congressman as a vote at
the North. A white man at the South had half as much more voice
in the legislation of the country than any man at the North. This had
been tolerated heretofore because of the compromises of the Constitution, and because it had been thought better to allow this great influence to slave property rather than run the chance of civil war.

But the civil war had occurred in spite of the compromises, and the
North had won. Now, the North insisted that no black man should
be represented unless he voted. It did not insist that black men
should vote, but that the white men of the South should not have the
power which slavery had given them, and which, by a singular effect
of the constitutional provisions, would be absolutely increased by the
results of the war and the abolition of slavery. For, if slaves were
simply emancipated and not enfranchised, and the number of representatives was to be apportioned to the number of the population,
exactly as at the North, the white voters would of course elect a
greater number of representatives than before. Until now, it had been
arranged that to the number of free persons should be added three-
fifths of "all others;" but as there would no longer be these "others,"
all being free, the Southern States would actually have their representatives increased by the two-fifths, and yet the small number of
whites in the southern States would elect them all.

It was manifestly unjust that the South should gain in political
power from its evil act, and therefore, after long discussion, Congress
determined to insist, that if the entire free population of the South
was to be represented, it should all vote; that the whites should not
vote for the blacks; or, if they chose still to exclude the blacks from

voting, that their number of representatives should be diminished pro-
portionately. In other words, that the voting population only should
be represented. This did not seem a very harsh stipulation to impose
upon a community which had rebelled against its Government, and
fought a long and bloody civil war, and been subdued—simply that in
readmission to a share in that Government, it should have no privileges
superior to those who had remained loyal, and finally had succeeded
in overthrowing the rebellion. Yet this, and the exclusion from
office of a few of those who had been most prominent in rebellion, was
all that Congress exacted.

The President, however, although he had enforced the abolition of
slavery upon the South, absolutely ordering the States to insert it in
their constitutions, was violently opposed to this necessary corollary of
emancipation—the rearrangement of representation. He strove to form
a new party, which should maintain his policy; and political strife at
once arose all over the land. The old friends of the rebels at the
North, those who had sympathized with them during the war, who had
done all that they dared to help them, but had been obliged in some
degree to veil their sympathies—now, finding they had the President
on their side, spoke out openly, and encouraged the southerners with
hopes of better terms than Congress offered them. This aroused the
rebellious spirit which had brought on the war, and all over the South
the good feeling which, under Grant's policy had begun to grow up,
under the President's was converted into hostility. From being pen-
itent, or at least submissive, the rebels became again blatant and
haughty. They declared themselves proud of their treason; they
insisted upon their rights under the Constitution—they who had
trampled on the Constitution, and who a few months before had
meekly sought their pardons! The whole tone of opinion and feeling
at the South was changed, and this reacted on the North, which, seeing the ancient defiant and insulting tone resumed—of those whom
it had so recently and severely chastised — became naturally indignant.

The worst of the rebels were not content with talk, but resorted to
deeds. In the State of Texas alone, Sheridan reported, officially, to
Grant, that over seven hundred Union whites and negroes were mur-
dered in one year, and no redress could be obtained. In no court of
a southern State could a Union man procure justice; no jury would
convict a rebel for any offence committed against a northerner or a
black; while at the same time, and in the same courts, suits were in-

9

stituted and decided against Union soldiers for damages done to property in the South during the war, by command of their officers. The southern papers teemed again with abuse of northerners; insults were offered to northern officers in southern cities by the men whom they had conquered, and the natural result occurred. The North resented the misuse that was made of its generosity. There were, it is true, many southerners who were sorry to see the strife rekindled, and who sought to control their misguided friends; but these were not sufficient to stem the current.

GRANT'S POSITION.

Grant had watched the course of events with great concern. With all his magnanimity, and even tenderness, for the vanquished, he had no idea of relinquishing one iota of the results that he had attained. As early as January, 1866, he issued an order, directing that no officer of the army should be sued, tried, or punished in any way by a civil court at the South for acts done during or since the rebellion. Complaints against officers or soldiers by civilians or ex-rebels must be lodged with their military superiors alone. Soon after this, he refused the Governor of Alabama permission to reorganize the militia of that State; he declared "he could not see the propriety of putting arms into the hands of the militia, until the rights of all classes of citizens should be perfectly secure, and the regular United States forces withdrawn." He also attempted to restrain, or at least rebuke, the extremely offensive and seditious tone which the southern press had begun to assume, and directed his subordinates to forward to his headquarters copies of any publications calculated to disturb the public peace, or manifesting a revival of the old rebellious spirit. In several instances rebel newspapers of this character were suspended by his orders. He was not among those who forgot that there had been a tremendous rebellion and a terrible civil war. He knew too well the cost that the country had paid to suppress that rebellion, and watched the change in the feeling and temper of the South closely, determined to do all in his power to avert further trouble in time. While the rebels were repentant and submissive, and thoroughly loyal, he was willing and anxious to do all in his power to win them with kindness, to restore them to prosperity, if not to power, and to ameliorate the miserable condition which they had brought upon themselves. But if they proved themselves unworthy of this treatment; if they began to boast of their treason; to annoy or distress Union men among them; to insult the Government which had spared them; he stood ready to administer fresh discipline as long as it was required, and to repress sternly the incipient symptoms of relapse.

There was, however, one portion of the community whom he never forgave, and those were the people at the North who had been false to the country in the hour of trial; those who had sympathized with the rebellion, who had croaked of disaster, who had rejoiced over the successes of treason, and done their best to dishearten the courage of the nation, while its defenders were spilling their blood in battle. Towards these men—the Woods, the Vallandighams, the Pendletons, the Clymers, the *Seymours* of the North—Grant was unrelenting. He could hardly treat them with civility when they approached him. He could forgive a rebel who fought with and for, as he supposed, the community in which he had been born; but those traitors, who deserted not only their country, but their State and section too, Grant could never pardon.

Some of them, because he had been magnaminous in victory, thought they could win him over to them, but he repulsed their over-tures with scorn. He rarely entered into politics, but declared openly that he hoped every soldier would vote always for Union men in pre-ference to politicians who had refused to supply men and money to carry on the war.

THE PHILADELPHIA CONVENTION.

But the President soon fell entirely into the hands of these people; he was surrounded by the most virulent, and this first led Grant to abate in his intimacy with Andrew Johnson, and to lessen his confi-dence in the President's opinions. While the contest between the President and Congress was at its height, a meeting of all those who supported Mr. Johnson's views was called at Philadelphia. This was attended by some excellent and patriotic men, who did not see clearly whither the views expressed by the President were carrying them; men sincerely anxious for harmony, who did not recognize the grow-ing revival of a treasonable spirit at the South, and who thought less restrictive measures than those proposed by Congress would best ac-complish reconstruction. But the great bulk of the men who had supported and carried on the war held themselves aloof from this attempt to inaugurate a new party. Even in that convention, how-ever, such men as Vallandigham and Wood were not allowed to speak;

though in more recent conventions, the former has nominated Presidents for the party that opposed the war.

A delegation was appointed by the Philadelphia convention to present resolutions of sympathy to the President, approving of his policy, rather than that of Congress. Mr. Johnson was extremely anxious to gain the countenance of Grant on this occasion. He wanted to throw the weight of Grant's immense popularity into the scale in his own favor. He knew by this time that Grant was much more strongly disposed to the Congressional scheme of reconstruction than to his own, and that he held firmly to the belief that the Executive was simply the instrument to carry out the laws; but he still sought to obtain Grant's presence and tacit approval, if he could not induce him to openly advocate the Presidential policy. Accordingly, on the morning of the arrival at the White House of the delegation from Philadelphia, the President sent Grant a note, requesting his presence at the Executive Mansion, but not stating the object of the visit which he desired. An invitation from the President is an order to a military officer; and Grant would have considered it necessary to obey, even had he known on what occasion his presence was desired; but of this he was not informed. He went to the White House, expecting to transact business with the President, and was ushered into the east room, where he found several hundred delegates paying their respects. The President made room for him at his side, and the delegates, after ·speaking to Mr. Johnson, all turned and shook hands with Grant. This was heralded all over the country as a proof that Grant approved the President's course, and had taken this means of showing his position.

CHICAGO TOUR.

Shortly afterwards, the President determined to make a tour to Chicago, and invited Grant to accompany him. It had now become apparent that the lines were to be drawn closely in politics, and that for Grant to accompany Mr. Johnson on this tour would be taken as an indication that he was a supporter of the President. Grant was especially anxious not to be regarded as a partizan; the elections were about to occur, and he was willing for the country to decide which policy it would adopt. He begged the President to excuse him from going on this trip. But Mr. Johnson repeatedly urged him to go, and finally, as a personal matter, renewed his invitation. It would, have been very indecorous in the general-in-chief to persist in refusal, and, very much against his will, he accompanied Mr. Johnson on the famous tour, which speedily became an avowed political enterprise, and one whose results were more disastrous to its originator than any other ever undertaken. Grant kept himself as much as possible in the back ground, and positively refused to make any speeches, although repeatedly called on; but, as he had foreseen, the advocates of the President declared that his presence during the trip was positive evidence of his adherence to the Presidential policy.

In July, 1866, he was promoted to a new rank, created expressly for him by Congress—that of General of the Army ; it was the highest ever known in the American army. The appointment was unanimously confirmed, and the commission issued at once. It was everywhere understood that this was done as a national and formal recognition of his illustrious services in the field.

THE ELECTIONS—THE COUNTRY DECIDES.

In the fall of this year, the elections for the succeeding Congress took place, the only question at issue being the policy of reconstruction. The campaign was vigorous, and the result unmistakably proclaimed the will of the people. By large majorities the country spoke in favor of the Congressional plan. The proposed amendment to the Constitution was submitted to the various State Legislatures at the North, and ratified by them, and Republican members of the Fortieth Congress were elected all over the land by increased majorities. It was, therefore, now certain that the President's policy was unacceptable to the loyal people of the country.

GRANT'S ADVICE TO THE SOUTH.

But Mr. Johnson was still far from submitting. He had opposed Congress, appealing to the people; but, when the people decided against him, he was as determined as ever. Grant, however, considered that *"the will of the people is the law of the land,"* and that it was the duty of every executive officer not only to submit, but to "take care that the laws be faithfully executed," no matter what his own opinions might be of the justice or even constitutionality of those laws. He now used every means to induce the southern people to accept the terms of reconstruction offered them by Congress—to adopt the constitutional amendment, and return in good faith to that Union which they had striven so hard to overthrow. His influence with Southerners had been great; none of distinction at this time ever was in Washington without visiting his house or his headquarters, and to all who came he proffered the same advice. Formal delegations from some of the southern States were sent to the capital, to take the opinion of public men there as to the propriety of accepting these terms. These delegations all saw Grant, who sometimes went out of his way to meet them, and to urge upon their members the importance of adopting the constitutional amendment. One of these interviews took place at the house of the Secretary of State, who was known to be opposed to the amendment, although it had been endorsed by the North, but who invited Grant to meet the delegation from Arkansas. Grant went, and spoke very plainly; he told the Arkansas members that he spoke as their friend; he assured them that the temper of the North was such that, if these terms were rejected, still harsher ones would be imposed. He argued, and plead, and besought them, for their own sakes, for the sake of the entire South, for the sake of the country, to conform to the situation, to recognize that they had been conquered, to yield frankly, to return to the Union; and assured them that a speedy reconciliation would ensure the lightening of all that was really onerous in the stipulations proposed.

Many important and sensible southerners agreed with Grant that it was the true policy of the South to submit to what it could not avert; but the President's influence was all thrown the other way. He assured those who had been rebels that a change would come in the temper of the North; he advised them not to accede to what was demanded; he promised them his influence, and finally was able to dissuade them from accepting the amendment. Every southern State rejected it. Not one but regrets that fact to-day.

THE MARYLAND MATTER.

About this time, political differences occurred in the State of Maryland, which threatened to create a collision between the State authorities and those of the city of Baltimore. The Democrats, who were, as usual, in league with those of the former rebels who still remained blatant and defiant, appealed to the President for armed assistance, and he made several communications to Grant, with a view of inducing Grant to order troops into the State of Maryland. But Grant replied, that there was neither necessity nor law for such a course. He feared that in the excited state of public feeling, which Mr. Johnson's course had aroused, the use of troops would provoke bloodshed, and that this might prove the spark of a conflagration that could not easily be suppressed. The law was positive on the subject, and the Administration was obliged to acquiesce in Grant's interpretation. Grant addressed the President in these words: "I cannot see the possible necessity for calling in the aid of the military *in advance of even the cause which is to induce riot.* The conviction is forced on my mind that *no reason now exists for giving or promising the military aid of the Government to support the laws of Maryland. The tendency of giving such aid or promise would be to produce the very result intended to be averted. It is a contingency I hope never to see arise in this country, while I occupy the position of general-in-chief of the army, to have to send troops into a State in full relations with the General Government, on the eve of an election,* to preserve the peace. If insurrection does come, the law provides the method of calling out forces to suppress it. *No such condition seems to exist now.*"*

But the President seemed very much chagrined that he could not induce Grant, on his own responsibility, to make the order. He took good care, however, to give no such directions himself. Grant went to Baltimore in person at the critical moment, and, seeing both parties, averted all danger, inducing them to leave the decision of their rights to the authority of the courts.

MEXICO—ATTEMPT TO DRIVE GRANT OUT OF THE COUNTRY.

His course in this matter, however, as well as his outspoken advice to the Arkansas delegation, had proven very plainly that he could not be induced to do anything in favor of the President's extraordinary views, outside of the letter of the law; and it was determined to supplant him. The Administration did not dare absolutely to remove from office the most popular man in America, especially when the office had been created especially for him. A plan was therefore concocted to get Grant out of the way, and to put Sherman, who, it was hoped, would prove more supple, in his place. Sherman had said and written several things which the President construed into an approval of his policy. So Grant was directed to order Sherman to Washington, but not informed of the reason for the order.

---

* See Ex. Doc., No. 57, Fortieth Congress, second session, pages 63 and following.

To fully explain the extraordinary proceedings which now took place, it is necessary to take a retrospect. The invasion of Mexico, by the French, during the existence of the armed rebellion, was undoubtedly undertaken in the interests of that rebellion ; and when our internal war was over, Grant, regarding the French occupation as only a part and parcel of the rebellion, was very anxious to compel the evacuation of Mexico. He did not think it would be necessary to resort to arms in order to accomplish this, but he believed that a threat of war, in case the evacuation were not immediate, would have the desired effect.

He urged repeatedly and earnestly upon the Government, that now was the time, while we had still hundreds of thousands of men in arms, to say to the Emperor of the French, that we could not tolerate the occupation of Mexico by a European power. Before our armies were disbanded, he ordered Sheridan, with a large force, to the banks of the Rio Grande, especially to watch the movements in Mexico, and with the hope that he could persuade the Goverment to call peremptorily upon France to withdraw. But the Secretary of State had no relish for such positive proceedings. They were not in accordance with his adroit diplomacy, and the frank, outspokenness of the soldier, was not so acceptable to the President as the wily machinations of the veteran politician. The President professed to wish to see the French leave Mexico, but he never followed Grant's advice in the matter. He never summoned France to leave, until he knew that her troops were embarking. Still Grant kept up for two years his anxious and earnest importunity on this subject. He spurred on the unwilling Government, and whatever was accomplished in this matter was due, in reality, to his pertinacity, and to the threat which the presence of Sheridan, with an army on the Rio Grande, constantly offered to Louis Napoleon. Besides this, Grant openly spoke in favor of his views—a course most unusual with him—and fostered, by every means in his power, the popular feeling against the French occupation. He constantly advised that arms should be supplied the Mexicans by our Government; he encouraged the Mexicans whom he saw, to hold out; and was, by far, *the most active and persistent friend of the Monroe doctrine in America.* It is not too much to assert, that it was this unintermitted effort and influence of his, that stimulated the Government and menaced the Emperor of the French, (who was well aware of Grant's feeling on the subject,) and that finally secured the evacuation of Mexico. But for this, the time-serving, procrastinating policy of the Secretary of State would have lasted till now, and the Empire of Maximilian would have still existed; the nucleus, perhaps, of a future rebellion, as it was, both during and long after the war, the nest of traitors and the abettor of treason.

The Administration, in its anxiety to get rid of such a loyal, law-abiding, and powerful patriot as Grant, bethought itself of Mexico, and determined to send him thither. Knowing his profound interest in the subject of Mexican independence, it was thought he would bite at the bait at once; and, as the country was also well aware of his sentiment, there would be excuse enough to veil their real motives, and account for the exile of the greatest of our soldiers. The movement was sudden. No peculiar interest in Mexico had been manifested by the Government for months; it was known that the French Emperor was tardily preparing to withdraw his troops; there was not the shadow of a real cause for the proposition; but all at once, in November, 1866, the President informed Grant that he meant to send him to Mexico. He was to go, not at the head of an army, but on a diplomatic mission, in connection with an obscure individual, one Colonel L. D. Campbell, who had recently been appointed minister to Mexico; but who, it was supposed, could not be confirmed by the Senate. There was no special object of the mission announced; Grant was simply to go to Mexico, and examine, as well as he could, into the state of affairs; he was given no powers or authority, not even that of an ordinary minister, and was not instructed or empowered either to make demands, or to back his statements with menaces or men. He was simply to give Lewis D. Campbell the "*benefit of his advice,*" "*in carrying out the instructions of the Secretary of State.*"*

The device was transparent to the far-seeing, honest man, and he promptly declined to go. This was in conversation with the President. But a day or two afterwards the President returned to the subject, and urged the embassy on Grant, saying he had sent for Sherman to take his place in the meantime. Congress was about to assemble, and the air was full of rumors that the President would refuse to aknowledge the validity of Congress, and attempt to disperse it by arms. Mr. Johnson had recently seemed to have peculiar designs in regard to Maryland. Grant remembered all this, and again declined to leave the country, this time in writing. After this, he was summoned

---

* See Ex. Doc., No. 57, Fortieth Congress, second session, House of Representatives, page 69.

to a full Cabinet meeting, where his detailed instructions were read
out by the Secretary of State, as if the objections and refusal had
been of no account. They were determined to make him go, whether
he would or not—*to drive him out of the country which he had saved.*
Grant was now aroused, and, before the whole Cabinet, declared his
unwillingness to leave. Whereupon the President, not answering
Grant, turned to the Attorney General, and asked him whether there
was any reason why Grant should not obey this order—whether he was
ineligible to the position in any way. Grant at once started to his
feet, and exclaimed, "I can answer that question, Mr. President,
without appealing to the Attorney General. I am an American citi-
zen, have been guilty of no treason or other crime, and am eligible to
any civil office to which any other American is eligible. But this is a
purely civil duty, to which you would assign me, and I cannot be compelled to undertake it. Any legal military order you give me, I will
obey; but this is civil and not military, and I decline the duty. No
power on earth can force me to it." The President and his ministers
were astounded and silent, and Grant left the Cabinet-chamber.

Even after this, copies of his instructions were forwarded to him
through the Secretary of War, who was directed to request him to
proceed to Mexico. He now wrote a second letter, declining most
positively the duty assigned him. But, meanwhile, Sherman had been
sent for, and had arrived. The country was rife with rumors of the
object of his coming; the Administration had to conjure up some
excuse for sending for him. The President, therefore, urged him to
accept the position of Secretary of War; but this Sherman peremptorily declined. So, after a day or two, Grant was directed to turn
over his instructions for the Mexican mission to Sherman, and Sherman was sent to Mexico with Campbell, while Grant was let alone.
Sherman accomplished nothing by his mission, as neither he nor any
one else expected he would; and, after a month or so, he returned.
For all that was done, he might as well have remained in St. Louis;
but it was necessary to save the credit of the Administration, and he
was made the scapegoat.

CONGRESSIONAL RECONSTRUCTION.

When it was definitely known that the terms upon which readmission to the Union was proffered to those who had been in rebellion had
been refused, although those terms had been submitted to the people

of the North, and by them overwhelmingly approved, Congress at once set about the work of reconstruction, whether the southern States agreed or not. It was not to be endured that the work for which so many lives had been spent, so much toil, and danger, and expense incurred, should be forfeited, because those who had caused all this expenditure were still recusant. There was no obligation on the loyal people to consult the rebels at all; the nation had won, and might dispose of its own; it had chosen to be lenient, to be more than lenient; it had taken none of the lives that were fairly forfeited; it had confiscated no property since the close of the war; it had even offered to allow those who had striven for its ruin, a share in the Government; but they had refused. Now, it was determined that the States should return, whether they wished it or no. They should be governed, and as the loyal people desired. The whole rebellious region was at once divided into five military districts, and military rule declared supreme in each. The commanders had power to remove any political officer, to set aside any State law, and were especially enjoined to see that the justice which the State courts had persistently denied to Union soldiers and Union men, white or black, should be impartially administered. This condition of affairs was to last until the States chose to return to the Union, under new and more unpalatable conditions than those which they had refused. It had become evident that the fruits of the war could only be secured by a free admission of the colored population to the right of suffrage. The entire rebellious portion of the southern people were determined that they would not submit to the terms proposed by Congress; but, by throwing open the ballot to the negroes, a majority could be obtained large enough to carry out the measures which the loyal people desired. It was accordingly decreed that the colored people should vote on equal terms with the white. The blacks had been staunchly loyal during the war, of which they were in so large a degree the cause; and there was no doubt that their sympathies and votes would be decidedly with the men who had freed them; with the Government and the nation, rather than with the faction which had held them in slavery, and warred against the country. The former rebels were still not disfranchised; with a long-suffering unparalleled in history, the Government, justly incensed as it was at their stiffneckedness and insolent defiance of those who had conquered them, still allowed them a voice in selecting that government and determining its policy; but it insisted that the blacks should share in proportion to their numbers. When State constitutions, in conformity with this condition of affairs, should be formed by this increased voting population, presented to Congress, and accepted by it, the military rule should cease, and the rebel States be admitted again to an equal share in the Government.

This is, in few words, the Congressional system of reconstruction, enacted by Congress in March, 1867; it was passed over the veto of the President, and, because of the President's known and pronounced opposition to it, a supervisory power over the military district command- ers was given to Grant. It was even proposed to make him supreme over the southern States, and independent of the President; but against this he advised in the strongest manner, as subversive of the princi- ples of the Government; and his counsels prevailed.

From this time, however, he entered upon one of the most difficult administrative positions that any soldier or civilian was ever called upon to fill. In a condition of affairs amounting to revolution; where an entire hostile population had to be controlled, while a recently- enfranchised one was to be enlightened and led upward; where the legislative and the executive branches of the Government were at open enmity; where the passions of a terrible civil war were yet not subsided; where an arbitrary military rule was established under a democratic and republican form of government;—he was placed amid all these contending interests and passions, to balance, and soothe, and direct, and influence all. A subordinate of the President, he was yet in some important respects declared independent of him; and it was made his duty by the law to carry out a policy which the Presi- dent sought by every possible means to thwart and destroy.

No statesman ever had so delicate or difficult a task before. To the performance of this task he brought great sagacity, untiring patience, unparalleled equanimity, persistency, purity, and a desire to do justice to all. He was able even yet to postpone the fiercest phase of hostility that was destined to appear between the President and the Congress; he strove to do nothing offensive to the former—to obey all his legal orders, to show him all the respect due his office—and at the same time to carry out the spirit of the laws, which he and every other officer of the Government was bound to obey; to protect the white and black Unionists at the South, while he treated rebels with mingled leniency and justice. He was, however, convinced that since these measures had been inaugurated by Congress, it was for the interest of the country that they should be successfully carried out. He believed that the old spirit of the war had revived at the South to such a degree, that strenuous repression of it was necessary. He advised the removal from office of all persons who were not really anxious to renew their allegiance to the flag; at the same time that he repeatedly urged upon Congress the remission of the penalties of treason in the case of those whose course proved that they were now really loyal. By this spirit his whole course was guided. He had no power (except in one or two particulars) to order the district commanders in the discharge of their civil duties, but he advised them constantly; and, with a single exception, they always asked and took his advice as orders.

PROGRESS OF RECONSTRUCTION.

Under his wise and really pacific management, the evil spirit at the South began to subside, murders were less common, justice was more frequent, the rebel population itself declared its satisfaction with military rule, its preference for this to any other government. Meanwhile, the registration of the new voters commenced, and all things went on smoothly. It seemed as if the reconstruction measures must succeed, and peace was to come at last to this distracted land. The rebels, finding that Mr. Johnson was powerless and the North determined, were submitting to the inevitable.

OPPOSITION OF THE PRESIDENT.

But now the President discovered some loopholes in the law through which he still might be able to frustrate the will of the representatives of the people. He had been left the power to appoint the district commanders. He had appointed them all — Sheridan, Schofield, Sickles, Pope, and Ord; all soldiers, who, before the war, were without any tinge of abolition sentiment; all men who, since the war, had evinced the strongest sympathy with the original magnanimous policy inaugurated by Grant. But all were men accustomed to obey the law; all strove heartily to carry out the laws of Congress under which they were appointed; and it was through their united endeavors, in a great degree, that the success of the reconstruction measures seemed likely to be ensured. The President, however, endeavored to thwart their action, and repeatedly obliged Grant to defend them. He took the position that the reconstruction acts were unconstitutional, and that, therefore, he was not bound to obey them. Grant held that only the Supreme Court could pronounce on this question of constitutionality or unconstitutionality; and that, till that tribunal should pronounce, all officers, from the President down, were bound to obey these laws. The Attorney General gave opinions in favor of many of the President's views, especially declaring that any person at the South who was willing to take the oath of allegiance should be registered as a voter. Congress had expressly directed that certain classes at the South should be excluded from the franchise. The President directed Grant to forward this opinion to the district commanders. He obeyed, but at the same time informed them that the law made them their own interpreters of their powers and duties; and as thePresident did not choose absolutely to direct him or them to act according to this opinion, they did not do so. Sheridan, who commanded the fifth military district, consisting of the States of Louisiana and Texas, was proceeding with his work with so much vigor, that unless his efforts were speedily arrested, it was evident he would soon succeed in bringing those States into the Union. The President, therefore, in the summer of 1867, determined to remove Sheridan, as well as the Secretary of War, who was the only member of his Cabinet now in harmony with the Union sentiment of the country.

SUSPENSION OF STANTON.

The President's avowed unwillingness to conform to the measures of Congress had been so great, that the national legislature, on adjourning in the spring, had left itself at liberty to meet again in July, if the action of the President rendered this desirable. There was no doubt on the subject when the time came. Congress met, and placed the subject of reconstruction still more completely in the hands of the General of the Army. It had been thought that Mr. Johnson would endeavor to remove Mr. Stanton, because of his sympathy with Congress, and a law had been passed, taking from the President the power to remove his Cabinet ministers without the consent of the Senate. The President had vetoed the bill, but it was passed over his veto, he declaring it unconstitutional, and threatening not to obey it; and after Congress again adjourned, he announced to Grant his intention to remove the Secretary of War, and to make Grant the successor of Stanton.

In this design the Government may have been actuated by a double motive. They saw the great and increasing popularity of the general-in-chief, and, perhaps, thought, by bringing him into a political situation, to entangle him, and lessen his influence with the people, and his probable chances as a Presidential candidate. But they were also anxious to secure the present prestige of Grant for their own unpopular course, although they knew full well how thoroughly Grant was in sympathy with the Congressional measures, and how many causes of difference had arisen between him and the Administration in this matter. The people, however, were not so well apprized as they. Grant had thought it his duty to his superior and to the country to conceal these differences from the public. He was anxious to overcome the President's obstinacy, and still hoped to avert some of the dangers which that obstinacy threatened to bring upon the land. Beside this, he wanted to avoid the indecorum of a dissension with his chief before the world. The country, therefore, was uncertain (in some degree) of Grant's position on these subjects; although to the President and his Cabinet, and to his subordinate officers, he had proclaimed his opinions again and again. Now, if the President meant to avail himself of this decent reticence which Grant had maintained, he could, by placing the general-in-chief in his Cabinet, give to himself, before the country, the sanction of the greatest name in America. But Grant at once protested against the removal of either Mr. Stanton or General Sheridan. He did this in conversation, when the matter was originally mentioned; but, after the interview was ended, he addressed the President a letter, marked "Private," in which he used the following words:

"On the subject of the displacement of the Secretary of War: His removal cannot be effected against his will without the consent of the Senate. It is but a short time since the United States Senate was in session, and why not then have asked for his removal, if desired? It certainly was the intention of the legislative branch of the Government to place Cabinet ministers beyond the power of executive removal, and it is pretty well understood that, so far as Cabinet ministers are affected by the 'tenure-of-office bill,' it was intended specially to protect the Secretary of War, whom the country felt great confidence in. The meaning of the law may be explained away by an astute lawyer, but common sense, and the views of loyal people, will give it the effect intended by its framers."

This delayed the President's action for a week or so; but on the 12th

of August, Mr. Johnson, acting in strict conformity with the provisions of the tenure-of-office bill, suspended Mr. Stanton from office
as Secretary of War, and appointed Grant *ad interim* in his stead.
He had first requested Mr. Stanton to resign ; but that officer declined,
stating that grave considerations of public duty impelled him to this
course.

When the President made the order appointing Grant, the Secretary urged the latter to accept, assuring him that the interests of the
country required it. Grant was well aware that his motives would be
misconstrued by many of his countrymen, but he felt that he might
be able, in the Cabinet, to prevent some of the other changes upon
which the President was apparently bent, and, perhaps, to avert dangers almost equal to those which the country had so recently incurred.
He had so often, and avowedly, and within the last two weeks so ex-
plicitly, and in writing, stated to the President his views on all subjects
connected with reconstruction, that there was no disguise on his part,
nor misconception on the President's, of Grant's motives in entering the
Cabinet. From the first day till the last of his service as Secretary
of War, he maintained, openly and earnestly, the opinions and the
position which his letters of August 1st and 17th indicate. For a few
days after his entrance upon his new duties, nothing was said about
the removal of Sheridan, and Grant began to hope that the removal of
Stanton would satisfy Mr. Johnson.

REMOVAL OF SHERIDAN.

But the rebels in Louisiana urged the matter strongly, and especially
insisted that unless the President acted soon, Louisiana would be reconstructed, and Congress triumphant. On the 17th of August, therefore, without further premonition, he directed Grant to issue an order
removing Sheridan, and substituting General George II. Thomas in his
stead. That sturdy patriot, however, had no idea of being brought
in to obstruct the laws of the land, and wrote at once in the most
urgent terms to request not to be substituted for Sheridan. Thereupon General W. S. Hancock was appointed, and he made no difficulty
in accepting the position.

In announcing these orders to Grant, the President invited any
remarks from the general-in-chief which he might choose to make,
and the general replied in his memorable and eloquent letter, in which
he used the following patriotic words:

"I am pleased to avail myself of this opportunity to urge, earnestly urge, urge in the name of a patriotic people, who have sacrificed hundreds of thousands of loyal lives, and thousands of millions of treasure, to preserve the integrity and Union of this country, that this order be not insisted on. It is unmistakably the expressed wish of the country that General Sheridan should not be removed from his present command. This is a Republic, where the will of the people is the law of the land. I beg that their voice may be heard. General Sheridan has performed his civil duties faithfully and intelligently. His removal will only be regarded as an effort to defeat the laws of Congress. It will be interpreted by the unreconstructed element in the South—those who did all they could to break up the Goverment by arms, and now wish to be the only element consulted as to the method of restoring order—as a triumph. It will embolden them to renewed opposition to the will of the loyal masses, *believing that they have the Executive with them.*"

A torrent of indignation broke all over the land from the friends of the Republic at the removal of Stanton and Sheridan; and many staunch friends of Grant did not hesitate to disapprove his course in entering Mr. Johnson's Cabinet. They considered that this step indicated that the great soldier was in sympathy with the policy of the President. Grant remained silent under the unmerited reproach, calm in the consciousness of having performed his duty; and in a short time the whole correspondence between the President, himself, and Mr. Stanton, was given to the country, in answer to several calls from Congress, and the position of Grant became established. To add the peculiar duties of a Cabinet officer to those with which Grant was already intrusted, by virtue of his position as General of the Army, and those imposed on him by the reconstruction laws, was to make him almost more powerful than the President, and to oppress him with still heavier and more complicated responsibilities than any he had yet incurred. But he was able, with wonderful sagacity, to act so as for a long while to seem to command the approbation of all, even of the adherents of the President. The following extracts from his correspondence with Mr. Stanton show his relations with the man whom he had superseded :

Grant to Stanton.

"SIR: Enclosed herewith I have the honor to transmit to you a copy of a letter just received from the President of the United States,

10

notifying me of my assignment as Secretary of War, and directing me
to assume those duties at once. In notifying you of my acceptance,
I cannot let the opportunity pass without expressing to you my appreciation of the zeal, patriotism, firmness, and ability, with which you
have ever discharged the duties of Secretary of War."

Stanton to Grant.

* * "You will please accept my acknowledgment of the kind
terms in which you have notified me of your acceptance of the President's appointment, and my cordial reciprocation of the sentiments
expressed."

GRANT AS SECRETARY OF WAR.

At the same time, Grant's letters to the President had sufficiently
explained to that functionary and to the country his sympathy with
the policy of Congress. But as he was now *ad interim* Secretary of
War, it was necessary for him to attend Cabinet meetings, and therefore to be present at many political discussions, for whose tendency
he had neither interest nor approbation. He therefore represented to
the President that, as he was only holding the office of Secretary of
War until another should be appointed, and that not by his own suggestion or desire, and as his legitimate position was that of General
of the Army, who might be compelled to serve under successive
Administrations, he should be excused from participation in the purely
partisan duties of a Cabinet minister. The President at first paid
no attention to his request, but subsequently Grant renewed it repeatedly, and at last was accustomed to remain at Cabinet meetings
only long enough ·to present his budget of papers as Secretary of
War, and transact the purely official business of his post. He was
then in the habit of retiring. This indicated very plainly to the
President, and the other members of his Administration, that Grant
was determined not to be considered one of them in purely political
matters.

He was sometimes requested to remain, and give his opinions on
matters not strictly within his province as Secretary of War, and when
he did so, those opinions were as pronounced as possible. The discussion of the constitutionality of the tenure-of-office bill, and other
measures connected with the reconstruction acts of Congress, was
frequent at such times, and Grant never left the President or his

Cabinet in doubt as to his position—that, until the Supreme Court should decide upon the constitutionality of these laws, the Government was bound to carry them out in spirit and in letter to the utmost of its ability.

RETRENCHMENT AGAIN.

But although he refrained as much as possible from participation in the political duties often expected from a Cabinet minister, he was earnest and energetic, from the start, in the performance of all functions pertaining legitimately to his office as Secretary of War. There were many abuses which had crept into the administration of the army during the protracted and costly civil war, which only an experienced army officer would be likely to recognize, and which a civilian might naturally suppose had existed as a part of the unwritten constitution of the service. These, and all other mismanagements, whether proceeding from neglect or downright misdoing on the part of subordinates or outsiders, Grant immediately set himself to work to correct. Retrenchment, as usual, was the first subject to attract his attention. The use of ambulances as carriages, at every headquarters in the army, had entailed an immense expense, unknown before the war. This practice was at once abolished, beginning at his own headquarters. The bureau of rebel archives had remained separate and distinct, under the charge of a civilian ; it was transferred to the Adjutant General's department, and the bureau for the exchange of prisoners was abolished, thus relieving the Government from the expense of a large number of clerks and civil employés. Immense quantities of stores had accumulated in the Quartermaster's department during the war, and had now become useless ; these were directed to be sold ; and the storehouses, for which great rents had been paid, were then given up. The volunteer officers yet remaining in the service were mustered out, in all but a few cases, where their services still seemed indispensable. The agency of the Freedmen's Bureau was restricted almost exclusively to officers of the army, so that the civilian employés were dispensed with, and the expenses of the bureau greatly reduced by this and all other means within his control. These various retrenchments were so important, that in his annual message to Congress, the President, no partial witness, declared that "salutary reforms have been introduced by the Secretary *ad interim*, and great reductions of expenses have been effected under his administration of the War Department, *to the saving of millions to the Treasury.*"

In fact, the useless offices that were cut off, the sinecures that were abolished, the extravagances that were curtailed, the system of rigid economy that was introduced, all indicated a decided administrative ability and honesty, that recalled the palmy days of the Republic, and afforded a happy augury of what would occur if he, who in a subordinate position was able to accomplish so much, should be elevated to the head of the Government. In Grant's report, as Secretary of War, he reduced the estimates for the expenditures of the Department in the ensuing year so greatly, that the report was distrusted by some, and the calculations were revised, when he brought down the estimates still further—to twenty-seven millions of dollars; and to this estimate the chairman of the Committee of Ways and Means (Hon. R. C. Schenck) has given his endorsement of its accuracy.

Meanwhile, the President's opposition to Congress continued, with all its evil results upon the country, inflaming the South with the hope of reacquiring all their old preponderance, till the ex-rebels openly talked of repudiating the national debt, and asserting their rights to all that they had forfeited by their treason. The whole country was kept in a state of agitation; business was disturbed, the finances became involved, good feeling between North and South had almost ceased, and, in the portion of the land where war had not raged, party spirit rose higher, if possible, than before the war. Every step the President took added to the excitement; every day he became more closely allied with those who had striven to overthrow the Government. He removed, first Mr. Stanton; then General Sheridan; then General Sickles, who was relieved by Canby; and Pope, who was relieved by General Meade. But both of the officers whom he thus placed in the position of district commanders at once began to carry out the laws in the spirit in which they were conceived. Only in General Hancock, who superseded Sheridan, did he find a solitary instance of a soldier who had made a reputation by his efforts against the rebellion and was willing to risk that reputation in the attempt to restore the rebels to power.

STANTON REINSTATED.

Finally, however, Congress reassembled, and some check was put upon the almost unbridled movements of the President. He was obliged, by the tenure-of-office bill, to report to the Senate, within twenty days after its meeting, the reasons for which he had suspended the Secretary of War. This he did, and the Senate, on the 13th of January, decided that the reasons were insufficient. By the express language of the law, the moment that the Senate decided this, Mr. Stanton was reinstated in his office. It had become evident, several days before, that the Senate would come to this determination, and, as soon as Grant was convinced of this, on the 11th of January, two days prior to the action of the Senate, he notified the President that he could not, without violation of the law, and subjecting himself to the penalties of fine and imprisonment, refuse to vacate the office of Secretary of War the moment Mr. Stanton was reinstated by the Senate.

He made this known to the President in person, as he had previously promised to do, in case he came to such a conclusion. The President, however, disputed Grant's views, and strove to induce him to change his intention. A long and earnest conversation ensued, each maintaining his own opinions vigorously; finally, it became late, and the President said he would see Grant again, to which Grant made no reply.

The next day was Sunday, and Lieutenant General Sherman being in town, Grant sent him to the President to urge the nomination to the Senate of some other person as Secretary of War, so that the Senate might act, and Mr. Stanton be relieved, and any unpleasant imbroglio avoided. The person proposed by Grant was Ex-Governor Cox, of Ohio, who had been a major general of volunteers during the war, and afterwards elected Governor of Ohio by the Republican vote, but who was now out of office. His position in politics was not so Radical as that of many of the President's opponents, and Grant hoped, if the President could be induced to nominate Cox, that the Senate would confirm him, and the difficulty might be bridged over. Sherman saw the President, urged this action upon him, and told him Grant was in favor of it; many of the President's advisers and friends concurred. Saturday, Sunday, and Monday passed, however, and the President did not act. But the Senate was not so dilatory. Late on Monday, the 13th of January, it resolved that the causes for removing Mr. Stanton were insufficient. The President, Stanton, and Grant were officially notified of that fact during the evening. Grant was at the President's levee that night, but had only formal, unofficial conversation with Mr. Johnson, having already notified him of what his own action would be.

On the morning of the 14th, Mr. Stanton took possession of the office of Secretary of War, and Grant notified the President in writing that he had received notice of the action of the Senate, and that his functions as Secretary of War *ad interim* ceased from the moment of his receipt of the notice. The President sent Grant a message, by the bearer of this letter, that he wanted to see him at Cabinet meeting that day. Grant obeyed the summons, and was addressed by the President as Mr. Secretary of War, and asked to open his budget. He at once reminded Mr. Johnson of the notification he had given him; whereupon the President stated that Grant had promised to hold the position of Secretary of War until displaced by the courts, or at least to resign, so as to place the President where he would have been had Grant never accepted the office. Amazed at this remarkable and unlooked-for assertion, Grant repeated what had actually taken place between himself and the President; though, to soften the evident contradiction his statement gave to the President's declaration, he said, alluding to an anterior conversation of himself and the President, the President might have understood him as he declared, namely, that Grant had promised to resign, if he did not resist the reinstatement. Grant, however, had not only never made such a promise, but had expressly told the President to the contrary, three days before. His anxiety, however, not to offensively contradict the President before his Cabinet, occasioned all of the subsequent difficulty. He was shocked and surprised at Mr. Johnson's assertions, and this natural indignation was also perverted by his enemy into an emotion of a very different nature, and with a very different cause.

CONTROVERSY WITH THE PRESIDENT.

The President now gave out to the public press statements of Grant's course, which directly affected his honor ; and, after submitting to this for a day or two, the general-in-chief addressed the President a letter on the subject, in which he complained of the " gross misrepresentations" which had been made, and asserted the facts as they have been given above. The President, in reply, reiterated circumstantially the charge which he had previously made in Cabinet meeting, and now declared that, in the presence of the Cabinet, Grant had acknowledged the truth of those charges ; and that he, the President, had read the offensive newspaper article to four of his Cabinet, who testified to the accuracy of its statements.

Grant had no option, when thus assailed, but to defend himself.

He had been attacked anonymously and through the public press, but, as was acknowledged, with the connivance of his superior; and when he wrote respectfully, but earnestly, to the President, that functionary took upon himself to endorse the most violent accusations in the newspapers against the personal honor of the General of the Army. Grant's reputation for veracity had never been impugned before by his bitterest enemies; the President had been frequently accused of deviations from truth; and the subordinate, now repeating all that he had formerly declared, reasserted the correctness of his statements in his own former letter, "*anything in the President's reply to it to the contrary notwithstanding.*" He then remarked: "And now, Mr. President, when my honor as a soldier and integrity as a man have been so violently assailed, pardon me for saying, that I can but regard this whole matter, from the beginning to the end, as an attempt to involve me in the resistance of law, for which you hesitate to assume the responsibility in orders, and thus to destroy my character before the country. I am in a measure confirmed in this conclusion by your recent orders, directing me to disobey orders from the Secretary of War—my superior and your subordinate—without countermanding his authority to issue the orders I am to disobey." "Mr. President, nothing less than a vindication of my personal honor and character could have induced this correspondence on my part."

In reply to this, the President wrote another letter, to the same effect as his earlier one, and appended to it letters of four of his Cabinet ministers. The Secretary of the Navy, addressing Mr. Johnson, declared that "The three points specified in that letter, giving your recollection of his conversation, are correctly stated," which amounts simply to a statement that the President *gave his own recollection* of the conversation correctly. The Secretary of the Treasury was less equivocal, and was not unwilling to put himself on record as saying, "Your account of that conversation, substantially, in all important particulars, accords with my recollection of it." Neither of these personages, however, complied with the written request of the President, "to state what was said in that conversation." The Secretary of State only attempted "to give the general effect of the conversation." His statement is long, but the gist of it is contained in the following words, referring to the President's declaration, that Grant had promised to agree to the President's wish: "General Grant did not controvert, *nor can I say that he admitted, the last statement.*" So, Mr. Seward was not willing to assert what the President had openly and repeatedly proclaimed, that Grant, before the Cabinet, had admitted the truth of Mr. Johnson's statement. Mr. Seward also suggested the explanation that Grant, on Monday, "did not expect the Senate to decide so promptly as to anticipate further explanation between himself and the President." The Secretary of the Interior answered in detail; but his statement in every important particular corroborated Grant. He said that Grant had declared in Cabinet meeting that "he came over on Saturday to inform the President of the change in his views, and did so inform him, and they continued to discuss the matter some time, and finally he left without any conclusion having been reached, expecting to see the President again on Monday." The Post-master General, however, unhesitatingly and in detail affirmed all that was important in the President's letter, in direct contradiction of General Grant, Mr. Seward, and Mr. Browning.

It will thus be seen, that on the question of veracity between the President and Grant, two of the Cabinet ministers supported the General of the Army; one was non-committal; another corroborated the President in general terms, and only one could be found who was willing, in detail, to stake his own reputation for truth against that of General Grant. That man was Alexander H. Randall.

TRIUMPH OF GRANT.

The result was now before the country. An honest soldier, noted for truth, impartiality, outspoken frankness, was pitted against a nest of wily politicians, against whom charges of untruthfulness had often been made before. The verdict was soon passed. Not a man in the land in his heart believed that Grant had deceived the President, and no one ventured to assert it except partisan maligners.

The effort to break down the man who had saved them during the war was repelled by the people, and recoiled on those who had made it. The animus was visible; unable to compel or induce the great soldier to coöperate in their schemes, it was sought to destroy his fair fame before the people, and the immense influence now shown openly to be cast against the policy of the President. Instead of this being accomplished, the loyal people rallied around him at once; he was made stronger in their hearts than ever before, and from this moment his nomination, and consequent election to the Presidency were secure. Mr. Johnson, by this very attack, elevated Grant higher than ever, and made him, beyond all doubt, his own successor in the Executive chair.

Those who had doubted Grant's adherence to the policy of Congress, were at once made certain, while those who were not partisans of Congress, and yet loved and honored the pure and noble man who had done as much for his country as even Washington, were as indignant at assaults on his honor as if their own had been attacked. To blot Grant's name, was to tarnish the glory of the country of which his name was now become a part. The malignity which could attempt this, it was seen, could not consist with patriotism ; and many who had believed at least in the integrity of the President, now were made sure that sagacity was not the only trait in which he was wofully lacking.

Grant hitherto had striven to keep aloof from politics, had taken no position in any party. He had his own views, and never scrupled to act on them or to express them when occasion arose, but he did this with no view of benefiting a party, as such. As General of the Army, he desired and hoped to act independently of every party ; but it was impossible any longer to pretend to act with the President, or to show him any but official respect. The lines were drawn so tightly, that whoever now was in Grant's position, necessarily drew towards him the Republicans. Grant's views, it has been seen, had long been in harmony with theirs, and the persistent hostility with which the President thereafter pursued him, raised him up hosts of friends among all who detested Andrew Johnson's course.

FURTHER PERSECUTION BY THE PRESIDENT.

Having failed in his endeavor to use Grant in order to keep Mr. Stanton out of office, the President now applied to Sherman. A second time he offered that general the position of Secretary of War, which Sherman again peremptorily declined. The President then conferred on Sherman the brevet of General, so as to make him equal in rank to Grant, when he might be ordered to supersede the General of the Army. Sherman was out of Washington when his name was sent to the Senate for confirmation, but he at once wrote and telegraphed to Senators that he did not wish the brevet, and his own brother opposed it in the Senate ; he was accordingly not confirmed. The President then sent in the name of General George H. Thomas for the same brevet, but that officer also peremptorily declined to be placed in antagonism with his chief or on the side of the President. He telegraphed promptly, declining the brevet, declaring that, under the circumstances, it was no compliment; thus this attempt also fell to the ground.

On the 12th of February, the President, still determining to bring Sherman to Washington, and thus provoke a rivalry, if possible, between the two greatest soldiers in the land, created a new military division, with headquarters at Washington, and ordered Sherman to its command. This, also, Sherman opposed with all his might, and the President was obliged to abandon the idea, lest he might make another enemy, for Sherman was determined not to be brought into conflict with Grant. Thereupon, Thomas was to be brought to Washington; but, when he declined the brevet in such uncompromising terms, he, too, was found unavailable. Still looking around for one to use, the President now hit upon Hancock, an officer who had distinguished himself under Grant, whom Grant had expressly nominated, first, for the position of brigadier general, and subsequently to that of major general, in the regular army; for whom the chief had always entertained a warm regard, which was shown on every occasion and in every suitable manner.

This officer, flattered with the idea of rivalling his chief, and also enticed by the chance, adroitly suggested, of himself becoming a Presidential candidate, fell into the snare. When he was sent to New Orleans to relieve Sheridan, he became the President's apt coadjutor, the friend of the rebels, the enemy of the Union men, and of the Congressional measures, to such an avowed extent, that a bill was introduced into Congress for the sake of mustering him out of the army; but Grant stepped in, with his potent influence, earnestly dissuaded Congressmen, and prevented the passage of the bill.

Hancock's salvation was thus due solely to Grant. But Hancock persisted in a course at New Orleans that finally compelled Grant to revoke one of his orders. This was done with all consideration for Hancock's feelings, and is an act occurring every day in the army. Nothing is more common than for a superior officer to countermand the orders of his subordinate; Hancock, however, at once resented the proceeding, and asked to be relieved. This happened in good time for the President, who acceded to Hancock's request, and appointed him to the command of the military division which Sherman and Thomas had spurned. Hancock accepted it, and, being placed in apparent hostility to Grant, at once became popular with the men he had fought during the war, and who now urged him strongly as a candidate for the Presidency; the bitterest rebels openly pressing his claims.

IMPEACHMENT.

And now came the most open and important step of the President. In direct opposition to the law forbidding such an act, he removed Mr. Stanton from the position of Secretary of War. The Senate passed a resolution, by more than a two-thirds vote, declaring that Mr. Stanton was still Secretary. The House of Representatives immediately impeached the President for the act, and he was tried before the bar of the Senate; the only President who had ever been summoned to this high court to answer for his acts. A large majority of the Senate found him guilty, but the Constitution required that two-thirds should so pronounce him, before he could be degraded from his office, and there lacked one vote of this requisite two-thirds; so the President remained in office.

NOMINATION OF GRANT TO THE PRESIDENCY.

Before the trial was completed, the representatives of the National Union Republican party met at Chicago, in convention, and the six hundred and fifty-two delegates, on the first ballot, unanimously nominated Ulysses S. Grant as their candidate for President. There had been no doubt for months that he would be the choice of the party, but this extraordinary unanimity was unparalleled in the political history of the country. The next night, an immense concourse of people assembled at his house, the overflow filling up the streets for a large distance outside, to congratulate him on his nomination. Governor Boutwell, of Massachusetts, was spokesman for the assemblage, and to him Grant replied in his first political speech:

" GENTLEMEN : Being entirely unaccustomed to public speaking, and without the desire to cultivate that power, it is impossible for me to find appropriate language to thank you for this demonstration. All that I can say is, that to whatever position I may be called by your will, I shall endeavor to discharge its duties with fidelity and honesty of purpose. Of my rectitude in the performance of public duties, you will have to judge for yourselves by the record before you."

A convention of soldiers and sailors had met at Chicago, at the same time with the Republican convention, and the former also, with

great unanimity, recommended Grant for the Presidency. On the
29th of May, a committee from this Soldiers and Sailors' Convention
presented him a formal address, to which Grant replied as follows:

"*Gentlemen of the Committee of Soldiers and Sailors:*

"I will say, that it was never a desire of mine to be a candidate for
any political office. It is a source of gratification to me, to feel that
I have the support of those who sustained me in the great rebellion
through which we have passed. *If I did not feel I had the support of
those, I would have never consented to be a candidate.* It was not a
matter of choice with me; but *I hope, as I have accepted, that I will
have your aid and support, from now until November, as I had it during
the rebellion.*"

There is little doubt that this appeal of their old chief to the Union
soldiers of the country, will be answered as warmly at the polls as it
ever was in the field.

The same evening, Grant was formally notified, by General J. R.
Hawley, the President of the Republican convention, of his nomination as President of the United States. He replied in these words:

"*Mr. President and Gentlemen of the National Union Convention:*

"I will endeavor, in a very short time, to write you a letter accepting
the trust you have imposed upon me. Expressing my gratitude for the
confidence you have placed in me, I will now say but little orally, and
that is to thank you for the unanimity with which you have selected
me as a candidate for the Presidential office. I can say, in addition,
I looked on, during the progress of the proceedings at Chicago, with
a great deal of interest, and am gratified with the harmony and unanimity which seem to have governed the deliberations of the convention.

"If chosen to fill the high office for which you have selected me, *I
will give to its duties the same energy, the same spirit, and the same will
that I have given to the performance of all duties which have devolved
upon me heretofore.* Whether I shall be able to perform those duties
to your entire satisfaction, time will determine. You have truly said,
in the course of your address, that *I shall have no policy of my own to
enforce against the will of the people.*"

Those who have perused this pamphlet, will agree that no better
pledge could be asked of Grant, than that he will give to the duties of

the Presidency the same "energy, spirit, and will" he has given to his duties heretofore. The country desires no more. Those who have read this pamphlet carefully, will also not be surprised at his promise to "have no policy of his own to enforce against the will of the people." They will have noticed how, throughout his entire career, this principle has governed him; how he has grown into his present position, and developed into his present attitude, in strict conformity to that will; how he was in harmony with the loyal people during the war; how he has striven to conform to their will since; and how it is solely in obedience to their will, that he stands before them a candidate for the Presidency to-day.

His letter of acceptance of the nomination is in these words:

"WASHINGTON, D. C., *May* 29, 1868.
"To General JOSEPH R. HAWLEY,
President of the National Union Republican Convention:

"In formally accepting the nomination of the National Union Republican Convention of the 21st instant, it seems proper that some statement of views, beyond the mere acceptance of the nomination, should be expressed. The proceedings of the convention were marked with wisdom, moderation, and patriotism, and, I believe, express the feelings of the great mass of those who sustained the country through its recent trials. I endorse their resolutions. If elected to the office of President of the United States, *it will be my endeavor to administer all the laws* IN GOOD FAITH, *with economy, and with the view of giving peace, quiet, and protection everywhere.* In times like the present, it is impossible, or at least eminently improper, to lay down a policy to be adhered to, right or wrong, through an administration of four years. New political issues, not foreseen, are constantly arising; the views of the public on old ones are constantly changing, and a purely administrative officer should always be left free to execute the will of the people. *I have always respected that will, and always shall.* Peace, and universal prosperity, its sequence, with economy of administration, will lighten the burden of taxation, while it constantly reduces the national debt. *Let us have peace.*

"With great respect, your obedient servant,
"U. S. GRANT."

The same spirit may here be traced which is apparent in the three speeches of the next President. Above all, a deference to the will of the people; a desire to be supported by those who were loyal during the war; and an extreme anxiety for peace. Those who are truly Republican, or truly Democratic, can agree to support him, who always has respected, and always will respect, the popular will; those who love their country, will sustain him whom they sustained during their country's trials; and those, North or South, who are anxious for peace, will find in this man's history full proof of his ability to conquer and preserve peace, and of his abiding desire to give *"peace, quiet, and protection everywhere."*

CONCLUSION.

CHARACTER AND POSITION OF GRANT THE SAME NOW AS DURING THE WAR AND AT ITS CLOSE.

Thus, then, Ulysses S. Grant is presented to this country for its suffrages at the approaching election. The man who entered the war four days after the President's first proclamation for volunteers, has not yet concluded his battle for the Union. He is opposed to-day by the same people, at the North and at the South, who were most active against him during the war. He is upheld by the same people who were his most urgent supporters while he led the armed forces of the Union. All the loudest rebels of the South are against him now; and at the North, all who predicted and desired defeat for him while he was in the field, predict and desire it now. Pendleton, Vallandigham, Wood, and *Seymour* are on the same side still, and destined, doubtless, to a new defeat, dealt by the same men who, at Appomattox, defeated Seymour, and Vallandigham, and Pendleton, as well as Lee.

The soldier who led the Union armies from Belmont to Richmond, who was so successful in every campaign, and so magnanimous after each success, is again in the field. He has not changed because it is a theatre for statesmanship upon which he now plays his part. His principles have been the same in peace as in war. He is still uncompromising with his foes in battle; he spares them not till they are conquered; he relaxes no legitimate effort now, as he did not before. If they persist, his harshness and determination continue; his sagacity reveals new measures, his skill devises new means, his genius works, out a way over and beyond all obstacles, his courage is never appalled his strategy never outwitted. The same qualities which brought him success on every theatre of operations in the land, which enabled him to conquer Floyd, and Pillow, and Beauregard, and Van Dorn, and Price, and Johnston, and Lee, in turn—these same qualities are exactly those which have been ripened since for civic purposes, and are as necessary for the statesman as they were for the soldier. The foresight, the patience, the energy, the calmness, the determination, the ability to select and use the talent of others, to control the unwilling, to direct vast masses, to influence and overcome would-be rivals, to raise up hosts of adherents, the fortitude under apparent disaster, the courage at unexpected crises, the fertility of resource, the comprehensive grasp of the situation of a continent, the equanimity under unexampled success which the soldier has manifested, are all traits that will be inestimable in the President.

These same traits have already been manifested in his semi-civil position since the war. He has displayed the same inflexible purpose against Andrew Johnson that he did against Robert E. Lee; the same wisdom in directing the governors of military districts which he showed when his generals were at the head of armies; the same calmness amid difficulties at Washington as at Donelson; the same ability to thwart the wily politicians in the Cabinet that he evinced in outmanœuvring Johnston and Pemberton at Vicksburg; the same devotion to duty; the same determination to accomplish the supremacy of those who fought for the country, mixed, all the time, with the same consideration for his adversaries, whenever they manifest a disposition to succumb. For his magnanimity at Appomattox is perfectly consistent with his position to-day. Had the rebels remained as submissive as they were then, had they not found injudicious friends—or, rather, interested and crafty allies—at the North, to incite in them a different spirit, and proffer them aid and counsel, Grant would still be willing to display the same generosity as then; but it must be a generosity which is based on the suppression of treason and the spirit which animated it. When treason lifts its banner again; when it proclaims that the rebellion was just, and glories in it; when its northern friends strive to commit the country to the ineffable disgrace of repudiating the debts incurred to put down rebellion; when rebels are welcomed, not as repentant and returning prodigals, but as gallant and glorious soldiers, whose sole achievements were aimed at the life of their country—then Grant is found just where he stood during the war—just where he stood at its close—at the head of all who maintain the supremacy of the Government, and inflexibly opposed to all who oppose it.

That this is the present position of the country needs no proof. When Horatio Seymour leads the hosts antagonistic to U. S. Grant, and is nominated at the urgent solicitation of Pendleton and Vallandigham, while his warmest supporters are Forrest and Wade Hampton, there can be no doubt. The people who pronounced the war a failure in 1864, not long before the surrender of every armed rebel in the land, have held another convention, in which they assailed the soldier who received those surrenders. Need more be stated? Does any patriotic man hesitate on which side to ally himself? Does any sensible man doubt that the result will be another victory by the same leader over the same enemy, as complete as that of Vicksburg, of Chattanooga, or of Appomattox Court House?